## "Are you worried that I might walk out on you?"

"Yes," Daniel admitted.

Rachel was shocked by the overwhelming sense of relief she experienced. "It isn't my place to leave," she pointed out. "That prerogative is all yours."

"Yes." Daniel didn't look at her. "But I don't want to leave. I know I have to prove myself to you again. I know it's going to take time. But I won't give in, Rachel...."

**MICHELLE REID** grew up on the southern edges of Manchester, England, the youngest of a family of five lively children. But now she lives in the beautiful county of Cheshire with her busy executive husband and has two grown-up daughters. She loves reading, the ballet and playing tennis when she gets the chance. She hates cooking, cleaning and despises pressing clothes! Sleep she can do without, and produces some of her best written work during the early hours of the morning.

### Books by Michelle Reid

# MICHELLE REID

## The Ultimate Betrayal

# Harlequin Books

TORONTO • NEW YORK • LONDON
AMSTERDAM • PARIS • SYDNEY • HAMBURG
STOCKHOLM • ATHENS • TOKYO • MILAN
MADRID • WARSAW • BUDAPEST • AUCKLAND

ISBN 0-373-11799-X

THE ULTIMATE BETRAYAL

First North American Publication 1996.

# CHAPTER ONE

THE telephone started ringing as Rachel was coming downstairs after putting the twins to bed. She muttered something not very complimentary, hitched six-month-old Michael further up her hip, and rushed the final few steps which brought her to the hall extension—then stopped dead with her hand hovering half an inch above the telephone receiver, her attention caught by the reflection in the mirror on the wall behind the telephone table.

God, you look a mess! she told herself in disgust. Half her pale blonde hair was hanging in damp twists around her neck and face while the rest of it spewed untidily from a lopsided knot to one side of the top of her head. Her cheeks were flushed, her light blue overshirt darkened in huge patches where bathtime for three small children had extended its wetness to her also. And Michael was determinedly trying to wreak its final destruction by tugging at the buttons in an effort to expose her breast. A greedy child at the best of times, he was also tired and impatient now.

'No,' she scolded, gently but firmly forestalling his forage by disentangling his fingers from her blouse. 'Wait.' And she kissed the top of his downy head as she picked up the telephone receiver while still frowning at her own reflection.

'Hello?' she murmured, sounding distracted—which she certainly was.

So distracted, in fact, that she missed the tense little pause before the person on the other end answered cautiously, 'Rachel? It's Amanda.'

'Oh, hi, Mandy!' Rachel watched pleased surprise ease the frown from her face, and only realised as she did so that she had been frowning. That brought the frown back, a perplexed one this time, because she had caught herself doing that a lot recently. 'Michael, please wait a little longer!' she sighed at the small boy grappling with her blouse.

He scowled at her and she sent him a teasing scowl back, her blue eyes alight with love and amusement. He might be the most bad-tempered and demanding of her three children, but she adored him just the same—how could she not when she only had to look into those dove-grey eyes and see Daniel looking back at her?

'Aren't those brats in bed yet?' Amanda sighed in disgust. She made no secret of the fact that she found the children an irritant. But then Mandy was the epitome of made-it-in-a-man's-world woman. She had no time for children. She was a tall, willowy red-head who strode through her highly polished life on a different plane from the one Rachel existed on. She was the sophisticate while Rachel was the comfortable, stay-at-home wife and mother.

She was also Rachel's best friend. Well, maybe that was going a bit far, she acknowledged. She was the only friend Rachel had kept in touch with from her school days. The only one of the crowd who now lived in London like herself and Daniel. The others, as far as she knew, had made their lives back home in Cheshire.

'Two down, one to go,' she told her friend. 'Michael wants feeding but he can wait,' she added, for the baby's benefit as much as Amanda's.

'And Daniel?' Amanda asked next. 'Is he home yet?'

Rachel detected more disapproval in her friend's tone and smiled at it. Amanda did not get on with Daniel. They struck uncomfortably hostile sparks off each other whenever they were in the same company.

So, 'No,' Rachel said, adding ruefully, 'So you're safe to call him all the rotten names you like. He won't overhear you.'

It had been meant as a joke, and not a very new one either. Rachel had always given Amanda leave to vent her opinion of Daniel when he wasn't around. It allowed her friend to get off her chest all those things she would have loved to say to his face only she never quite had the courage to. But this time just an odd silence followed the invitation, and Rachel felt a sudden and unaccountable tension fizz down the line towards her.

'Is something wrong?' she asked sharply.

'Damn,' Mandy muttered. 'Yes. You could say that. Listen, Rachel. I'm going to feel an absolute heel for doing this, but you have a right to——'

Just then, a pair of Postman Pat pyjamas came gliding down the stairs, the small figure within making out he was a fighter pilot, firing his forward guns. Michael shrieked with glee, his eyes lighting up as he watched his big brother come hurtling down towards them.

'Drink of water,' the pilot informed the questioning look in his mother's eyes as he reached the hallway, and flew off in the direction of the kitchen.

'Look——' Mandy sounded impatient '—I can hear you're busy. 'I'll call you back later—tomorrow maybe. I——'

'No!' Rachel cut in quickly. 'Don't you dare ring off!' She might be distracted, but not so much that she hadn't picked up on the fact that whatever Mandy wanted to say was important. 'Just hang on a moment while I sort this lot out.'

She put the receiver down on the table then went after her eldest son, her long, beautifully slender legs moulded in white Lycra leggings which finished several inches above white rolled-down socks and white trainers. She was not tall, but she was incredibly slender and her figure was tight—surprisingly tight considering the fact that she'd carried and borne three children. But then she worked out regularly at the local sports centre—swimming, aerobics, the occasional game of badminton when she could find the time.

'Caught you red-handed!' she accused her six-year-old, who had his hand lost in the biscuit barrel. Rachel sent him a fierce look while he went red, then sighed an impatient, 'Oh, go on then—and take one for Kate—but no crumbs in the beds!' she called after him as Sammy shot off with a whoop of triumph before she could change her mind.

The kitchen was big and homely, big enough to house the netted play-pen hugging one corner of the room. She popped Michael into it and gave him something messy to suck at while she went back to the phone.

'Right,' she said, dragging the twisted telephone cord behind her as she went to make herself comfortable on the bottom stair. 'Are you still there, Mandy?'

'Yes.' The answer was gruff and terse. 'Why don't you employ someone to help you with those kids?' Mandy asked irritably. 'They're an absolute pain in the neck sometimes!'

'I'll tell Daniel you said that,' Rachel threatened, not taking offence. So Mandy was not the maternal type; she could accept that. Rachel was very maternal, and was not ashamed to admit it. 'And we do employ help,' she defended that criticism. 'It's just that I like the house to myself in the evenings, that's all. Live-in help feels as though you've got permanent guests. I can't relax around them.'

'Become any more relaxed,' Mandy mocked acidly, 'and you'll be asleep! For goodness' sake, Rachel! Will you stop emulating Sleeping Beauty and wake up?'

'Wake up to what?' She frowned, totally bewildered as to why Mandy felt this sudden need to attack her.

A harsh sigh rattled down the line to her eardrum. 'Rachel,' she said, 'where is Daniel tonight?'

The frown deepened. 'Working late,' she answered.

'He's been doing a lot of that recently, hasn't he?'

'Well, yes—but he's been very busy with that take-over thing with Harveys. You know about it, don't you?' she prompted. 'I'm sure I heard you both discussing it the last time you came to dinner...'

'The Harvey thing was over months ago, Rachel!' Mandy sighed.

Months? Had it really been months since Mandy had come to dinner? Rachel pouted, thinking back. Michael had been about—three months old, she recalled. That was three months ago! My God, where had the days, weeks—months gone to?

'Hey!' she exclaimed. 'You'll have to come to dinner again soon. I hadn't realised it was so long since I'd seen you! I'll talk to Daniel and see which night would be——'

'Rachel!' The sheer exasperation in Mandy's voice cut her short. 'For goodness sake—I didn't call you to wheedle a dinner invitation out of you! Though your dinners are worth attending when you bother to put one on,' she added, with yet more criticism spicing her tone. 'Not that I know how you find the time, what with a house and three crazy kids to take care of, not to mention a selfish swine like...'

She was off on her usual soap-box, Rachel acknowledged, switching off. Mandy hated the way Rachel liked to run her home virtually single-handed, and she thought Daniel contributed little or nothing. She did not under-

stand how busy he was, how hard it had been for him
to scramble his way to the top and support a young
family at the same time. Nor did she understand that
Rachel did not mind the long hours he had to work, that
she understood that he was doing it for them, herself
and the children, for their future security.

'...and I just can't let it go on any longer without
telling you, Rachel. You are my friend, after all, not
him. And it's time someone woke you up to what's going
on under your very nose...'

'Hey, back up a little, will you?' Rachel had switched
her attention back to what Mandy was saying only to
find she had completely lost the thread of the conversation. 'I think I missed something there along the way.
What's going on right under my nose that you think I
should know about?'

'See?' Mandy cried impatiently. 'There you go again!
Switching off when someone is trying to tell you something important. Wake up, for God's sake, Rachel. Wake
up!'

'Wake up to what?' Like Mandy, she was beginning
to get impatient herself.

'To that bastard you're married to!' Mandy cried.
'Dammit, Rachel—he's playing you for a fool! He isn't
working late. He's out with another woman!'

The words cracked like a whip, bringing Rachel jerking
to her feet. 'What, tonight?' she heard herself say
stupidly.

'No, not tonight in particular,' Mandy answered
heavily, obviously thinking the question as stupid as
Rachel thought it. 'Some nights,' she adjusted. 'I don't
know how often! I just know that he is having an affair,
and all of London seems to know about it except for
you!'

Silence. Rachel was having difficulty functioning on
any conscious level. Her breath was lying frozen inside

her lungs, as pins and needles—like a deadening drug administered to ward off impending shock—gathered in her throat and made their tingling way down to her feet.

'I'm so sorry, Rachel...' Sensing her shock, Mandy's voice softened and became husky. 'Don't think I'm enjoying this, no matter how...' She had been going to say how much she resented Daniel and would enjoy seeing the mighty fall. But she managed to restrain herself. Mandy disliked Daniel. Daniel disliked Mandy. Neither of them had ever made a secret of the fact that they put up with each other only for Rachel's sake. 'And don't think I'm telling you this without being sure of my facts,' she added defiantly to Rachel's continuing silence. 'They've been seen around town. In restaurants—you know—being too intimate with each other for a business relationship. But worse than that, I've seen them with my own eyes. My latest has a flat in the same building as Lydia Marsden,' she explained. 'I've seen them coming and going...'

Rachel had stopped listening. Her mind had turned entirely inwards, seeing things—pointers that made everything Mandy was saying just too probable to be dismissed as malicious gossip. Things she should have picked up on weeks ago, but she had been too busy, too wrapped up in her own hectic routine to notice, too trusting of the man whose love for herself and the children she had never questioned.

But she was seeing now. His frequent grim moods recently. The way he snapped at her and the children, the many times he had remained downstairs in his study working instead of coming to bed with her—making love with her.

Sickness swam like a wave over her, making her sway, close her eyes, see other times when he had tried to make love with her only to find her too tired and unresponsive. Weeks—months—of bitter frustration when she had been willing enough to give but he had been unwilling to take without knowing he was giving back in return.

But she'd thought they'd sorted that problem out! She'd thought over the last week or two—since Michael had been sleeping through the night and she had been feeling more rested—that everything was getting back to normal again.

And it was only a few nights ago that they had made love so beautifully that Daniel had trembled in her arms afterwards...

God...!

'Rachel...'

No! She couldn't listen to any more. 'I have to go,' she said huskily. 'Michael needs me.' Couldn't, because she was remembering one other pointer that was far more damning than any weak points of irritability or even poor sexual performances! She was remembering the delicate scent of an expensive perfume emanating from one of his shirts one morning as she prepared it for washing. It had clung to the fine white cotton, all over it. The collar, the shoulders, the two front sections. It had been the same delicate scent she had smelled but not quite picked up on each time she had kissed him when he came home at night—on his late nights. On his lean cheek. In his hair.

Fool!

'No—Rachel, please wait. I——'

The receiver dropped noisily on to its rest and she sank, leaden-bodied, back on to the stairs. Seeing Daniel. Daniel with another woman. Daniel having an affair. Daniel making love, drowning in another woman's...

She retched nauseously, a hand going up to cover her mouth, turning into a white-knuckled fist to press her cold and trembling lips painfully against her clenched teeth.

The phone began ringing again. A tired cry coming from the kitchen joined the shrill sound, and she stood up, a strange kind of calmness settling over her as she first picked up the receiver, then dropped it immediately back on its rest. Then, with that same odd calmness which actually spoke of reeling shock, she lifted it off again and left it off, then walked towards the kitchen.

Michael went straight to sleep after his feed. He curled himself up into his habitual ball with his padded bottom stuck up in the air and his small teddy tucked beneath his chubby cheek. Rachel stood for a long time just staring down at him—not really seeing him, not seeing anything much.

Her mind seemed to have gone a complete blank.

She checked the twins' rooms as she passed by. Sammy was fast asleep with his covers kicked off as usual, arms thrown out across his pillow in abandonment. She bent to drop a soft kiss on her eldest son's cheek before gently pulling the covers over him. Sam was more like his father than the other two, dark-haired and determined-chinned. Tall for his age, too, and sturdy. Daniel had looked like him at that age; she had seen snaps of him in his mother's photograph album. And Sam showed a stubbornness of purpose in that six-year-old face—just like his adored father.

Her heart wrenched, but she ignored the ugly feeling, turning instead to go to the other room where she stood staring down at the sleeping figure of her daughter. Kate was a different proposition entirely from her twin. You could come into this room in the morning almost guaranteed to find her sleeping in exactly the same position you had left her in the night before. Kate, with her silky hair like sunshine on her pillow. The apple of her father's eye. She could wheedle more out of Daniel than anyone else in the family could. He openly and unashamedly adored his blue-eyed princess. And the precocious little madam knew it—and exploited it to its fullest degree.

Would Daniel so much as consider doing anything which could hurt his little girl? Or lower his stature in the eyes of his adoring eldest son? Would he dare place all of this in jeopardy over something so basic as sex?

Sex? A terrifying shiver went skittering down her spine. Maybe it was more than sex. Maybe he couldn't help himself. Maybe it was love—the real thing. Love. The kind of love men were willing to betray everything for.

Maybe this was all just a stupid lie. A dark and cancerous bloody lie! And she was doing him the worst indignity of all by even considering it as the truth!

Then she remembered the perfume. And the times he had stayed out all night—blaming it on the Harvey contract.

The damned Harvey contract.

She reeled away and walked blindly out of Kate's room and across the landing into their bedroom where, only last week, they had found each other again. Made love beautifully for the first time in months.

Last week. So what had happened last week to make him suddenly turn to her again? She had made an effort; that was what had happened. She'd been worried about the way their relationship was going, and she'd made an effort. Sent the children to stay with his mother for the night. Cooked his favourite meal, laid the table with their best china and lit candles, and greeted him home in a slinky black dress and with a kiss that promised so much...

So much, in fact, that she'd not even noticed the clenching of his jaw and the sudden twitch of that little nerve beside his mouth which was always a dead giveaway that he was labouring under severe stress. But she noticed it now, with aching hindsight. She closed her eyes tightly in the silence of their bedroom and saw his lean face clench, his tanned skin pale, that little nerve begin to work as she wound her arms around his neck and leaned provocatively against him.

God. The nausea came back, almost overwhelming her, and she stumbled blindly out of the room and down the stairs to their sitting-room, seeing so much—so much that she had been foolishly blind to until now—that she was barely aware of what she was doing.

The tension with which he had held her shoulders, trying to put some distance between them. The pained bleak look in his grey eyes as he had stared down at her inviting mouth. The sigh which had rasped from him and the shudder which had shaken him when she'd murmured, 'I love you, Daniel. I'm so sorry I've been such a pain to live with.'

He'd closed his eyes tightly, swallowed tightly, clenched his lips, and clenched his hands on her shoulders until she'd actually winced in pain. Then he'd pulled her close, hugged her to him, burying his face in her throat, and said not a word, not a single word. No answering apology, no answering declaration of love. Nothing.

But they had made love beautifully, she remembered now, with an ache which echoed deep into her being. Whatever else Daniel was getting from this other woman, he could still want her with a passion no man could fake—surely?

Or could he? she wondered now. What did she know of men and how their sex-drives worked? She had been just seventeen when she met Daniel. He had been her first lover—her only lover. She knew nothing—nothing about men.

. Not even her own husband, seemingly.

Her eye was caught by her own reflection in the mirror set above the white marble fireplace, and she stared numbly at herself. She looked pale, she noted, a trifle tense around the mouth, but otherwise normal. No blood evident. No scars. Just Rachel Masterson *née* James. Twenty-four years old. Mother. Wife—in that order. She smiled bitterly at that. Facing the truth of it in a way she had never allowed herself to do before.

You wanted him, she told her reflection. And my God, you got him—and all in the space of six short months, too! Not bad going for a sweet naïve seventeen-year-old. Daniel had been all of twenty-four. Far too worldly-wise, surely, she mocked her reflection cynically, to be caught out by the oldest trick in the book!

Then the cynicism left her, because it had not been a trick, and she had no right denigrating herself by calling it one. She had been seventeen and utterly innocent when she met Daniel at her very first visit to a real nightclub, with a crowd of girls from school who thought it hilarious that she was frightened they would ask her her age and discover she was not old enough to enter their establishment.

'Come on, Rachel!' they'd mocked her. 'If they ask you, you lie, like we do!' And they had given her a new date of birth which she repeated over and over to herself until she was safely inside the glittering dimness of the nightclub. And even then she had jumped like a terrified rabbit every time someone so much as brushed by her, half-expecting to be thrown out by one of the big burly bouncers dotted around the place. Then, slowly, she had relaxed, begun to enjoy herself along with the rest of them, dancing to the disco music and sipping white wine and feeling less inhibited as the evening went on.

She was aware of Daniel from the moment he stepped into the club. He carried that kind of charisma with him. A big, lean man with neat dark hair and the kind of clean good looks film stars were made of. The others noticed him too, and giggled when he seemed to be taking an inordinate interest in their dancing group. But it was Rachel he was looking at. Rachel with her long, pale blonde hair billowing in its natural spiralling curls around her shoulders and pretty face, expertly made-up by the far more experienced Julie, and her slender body encased in one of Julie's tight black mini-skirts and a red cropped vest top which gave tantalising glimpses of her flat stomach as she gyrated to the disco music. If her parents had seen her dressed like that, they'd have died of horror. But she had been staying with Julie while her parents went off to visit relatives that weekend, and they had no idea what their only child, born very late in their lives, was up to while they were away.

And it was to Rachel that Daniel came when the music changed to a lazy smooch, his hand light on her shoulder as he turned her to face him, his smile, like the rest of him, smooth, confident, charismatic. Aware of the other girls' envy, she let him take her in his arms without a word of protest, could still remember those first tingles of shy awareness that fizzed up inside her at his touch, his closeness, the hard smooth line of male brushing against soft and sensitive female.

They danced for ages before he spoke. 'What's your name?' he asked simply.

'Rachel,' she told him, shy-eyed and breathless. 'Rachel James.'

'Hello, Rachel James,' he murmured. 'Daniel Masterson,' he announced himself. Then, while she was still absorbing the sexy resonance of his beautifully modulated voice, he slid his hand beneath the cropped top, making her gasp at the hot stinging sensation of his smooth touch against her bare skin, and pulled her closer.

He made no attempt to kiss her, or talk her into leaving with him instead of her friends. But he did take her telephone number and promised to call her soon, and she spent the next week camped by the phone, waiting— yearning for him to call.

He took her for a drive on their first real date. He drove a red Ford. 'Firm's car,' he explained, with a wry smile she never quite understood. Then gently, but with an intensity which kept her on the edge of her seat with breathless anticipation, he made her talk about herself. About her family, her friends. Her likes and dislikes, and her ambitions to take art at college with a view to going into advertising. He frowned at that, then quietly asked her how old she was. Unable to lie, she flushed guiltily and told him the truth. His frown deepened, and he was rather quiet after that while she chewed on her bottom lip, knowing achingly that she'd blown it. Which seemed to be confirmed when he took her back home and just murmured an absent goodnight as she got out of the car. She'd been devastated. For several days she'd barely eaten, could not sleep, and was in dire danger of wasting away by the time he called her again a week later.

He took her to the cinema that night, sitting beside her in the darkness staring at the big screen while she did the same, only without seeing a single thing, her attention fixed exclusively on his closeness, the subtle tangy smell of him, his hard thigh mere inches away from her own, his shoulder brushing against hers. Dry-mouthed, tense, and terrified of making a single move in case she blew it a second time, she therefore actually cried out when he reached over and picked up one of her hands. His expression was grave as he gently prised her fingers out of the white-knuckled clench she had them in. 'Relax,' he murmured. 'I'm not going to bite you.'

The trouble was, she'd wanted him to bite. Even then, as naïve as they came and with no real idea of what it meant to be with a man, she had wanted him with a desperation which must have shown in her face, because he muttered something and tightened his grip on her hand, holding it trapped in his own while he forced his own attention back to the film. That night he kissed her hard and hungrily, the power of it taking her to the edge of fear before he drew angrily away and made her get out of the car.

The next time he took her out it was to a quiet restaurant, where his eyes lingered broodingly on her through the meal while he told her about himself. About his job as a salesman for a big computer firm which, by the nature of the job, meant he travelled all over the country touting for new business and could mean his being out of the area for weeks on end sometimes. He told her of his ambition to own his own company one day. How he dabbled in stocks and shares with his commission and lived on a shoe-string to do it. He spoke levelly and softly so that she had to lean forward a little to catch his words, and all the time his eyes never left her face, not just brooding, but seeming to consume her, so by the time he drove her home that night she was in danger of exploding at the sexual tension he had developed around them both. Yet still it was just the one hungry kiss before he was sending her into the house and driving away. It went like that for perhaps half a dozen more dates before eventually, inevitably, she supposed, his control snapped and, instead of taking her to the cinema as they had planned, he took her to his flat.

After that, they rarely went anywhere else. Being alone together, making love together, became the most important thing in her life. Daniel became the most important thing in her life, over her A-levels, over her ambitions, over the disapproval her parents made no bones about voicing but which made no difference to the way she felt.

Three months later—and after he had been away in London for almost two weeks—she had been waiting for him at his flat door when he returned.

'What are you doing here?' he asked, and it was only now, almost seven years later, that she realised he had been far from pleased to find her there. His face had been tired and tense—just as it had looked over these last few months, she thought, on another pained realisation.

'I had to see you,' she'd explained, slipping her hand trustingly into his as he walked into the flat. Inevitably they had made love, then she made some coffee while he showered and they drank in silence, he lounging in a lumpy old easy-chair wearing only his terry bathrobe, she curled at his feet between his parted knees as she always was.

It was then she had told him she was pregnant. He hadn't moved or said anything, and she had not looked at him. His hand had stroked absently at her hair and her cheek rested comfortably on his thigh.

After a while, he had sighed, long and heavy, then bent to lift her on to his lap. She had curled into him there, too. Like a child, she thought now. As Kate does when she goes to her daddy for love and comfort.

'How sure are you?' he had asked then.

'Very sure,' she had answered, snuggling closer because he was the axis her whole world turned upon. 'I bought one of those pregnancy test things when I missed my period this month. It showed positive. Do you think there could be a mistake?' she had asked guilelessly then. 'Shall I go and get a proper test from the doctor before we decide what to do?'

'No.' He had rejected that idea. 'So, you're only just pregnant. I wonder how that happened?' he had pondered thoughtfully.

That made her chuckle. 'Your fault,' she had reminded him. 'You're supposed to take care of all that.'

'So I was and so it is,' he had conceded. 'Well, at least we have time to get married without the whole town knowing why we're having to do it.'

And that had been it. The decision made as, really, she had expected it to be. With Daniel making all the arrangements, shielding her from any unpleasantness, handling her parents and their natural hurt and disappointment in her.

Again, it was only now, seven years later, that she took the words he had spoken and looked at them properly. 'We have time to get married without the whole town knowing why we're having to do it' he had said. And it hit her for the first time that Daniel would not have married her otherwise.

She had trapped him. With her youth, her innocence, with her childlike trust and blind adoration. Daniel had married her because he felt he had to.

Love had never come into it.

The sound of a key turning in the front door lock brought her jolting back to the present, and she turned, feeling oddly calm, yet lead-weighted, to glance at the brass carriage-clock sitting on the sideboard. It was only eight-thirty. Daniel had not been due home for hours yet. A business dinner, he'd called it. Now she bitterly mocked that excuse as she went to stand by the open sitting-room door.

His back was towards her. She could see the tension in him, in his neck muscles and in the stiffness of his shoulders beneath the padding of his black overcoat.

He turned slowly to send her a brief glance. She looked at his face, saw the lines of strain etched there, the greyish pallor. He moved his gaze to where the phone still lay off its rest and went over to it, putting his black leather briefcase down on the floor before picking up the receiver. His hand was trembling as he settled it back on its rest.

Mandy must have called him. She would have panicked when Rachel refused to answer the phone, and rung Daniel to tell him what she had done. Rachel would have liked to have listened in to that conversation, she decided. The cut and parry of confession, accusation, condemnation and defence.

He looked back at her through eyes heavily hooded by thick dark lashes, and she let him have his moment's private communion as he ran that gaze over the mess she must look. Then, without a word, she turned and went back into the sitting-room.

He was guilty. It was written all over him. Guilty as sin.

# CHAPTER TWO

SEVERAL minutes passed by before he joined her. Minutes he needed, to compose himself for what was to come, while she sat patiently waiting for him.

Strangely, she felt incredibly calm. Disconnected almost. Her heart was pumping quite steadily, and her hands lay relaxed on her lap.

He came in—minus his overcoat and jacket, his tie loosened around his neck and the top few buttons of his crisp white shirt tugged undone. He didn't glance at her but made straight for the drinks cabinet where his usual bottle of good whisky waited for him.

'Want one?' he asked.

She shook her head. He must have sensed her refusal because he didn't repeat the enquiry, nor did he look at her. He poured himself a large measure, then came to drop down in the chair opposite her.

He took a large gulp at the spirit. 'Loyal friend you've got,' was his opening gambit.

Loyal husband, she countered, but didn't bother saying it.

His eyes were closed. He had not looked directly at her once since coming into the room. His long legs were stretched out in front of him, whisky glass held loosely between both sets of fingers—long, strong fingers, with blunted nails kept beautifully clean. Like the rest of him, she supposed: long-limbed, strong-bodied and always kept scrupulously clean. Good suits, shoes, hand-made shirts and expensive silk ties. His face was paler than usual, strain finely etched into his lean bones, but it was

23

still a very attractive face, with clean-cut squared-off lines to complement the chiselled shape of his nose and slim, determined mouth. Thirty-one now—going on thirty-two—he had always been essentially a masculine kind of man, but through the years other facets of his character had begun to write themselves into his features: an inner strength which perhaps always came with maturity, confidence, a knowledge of self-worth. The signs of power and an ability to wield it efficiently all had a place in his face now—nothing you could actually point to and say, You have that because you're successful and know it, but just a general air about the man, which placed him up there among the special set.

And controlled, she realised now. Daniel had always possessed an impressive depth of self-control, rarely lost his temper, rarely became irritated when things did not quite go his way. He had this rare ability to look at a problem and put aside its negative sides to deal only with the positive.

Which was probably what he was doing now—searching through the debris of what one phone call had done to his marriage and looking for the positive aspects he could sift out from it.

That, she supposed, epitomised Daniel Masterson, head of Master Holdings, an organisation which had over the last few years grown at a phenomenal pace, gobbling up smaller companies then spitting them out again as better, far more commercially profitable appendages to their new father company.

And he had done it all on his own, too. Built his mini-empire by maintaining that fine balance between success and disaster without once placing his family and what he had got for them at risk. He had surrounded her with luxury, cherished her almost—as a man would a possession he had a sentimental attachment to.

'What now?' he asked suddenly, lifting those darkly fringed eyelids to reveal the dove-grey beauty of his eyes to her.

So, he wasn't going to try denying it. Something inside her quivered desperately for expression, but she squashed it down. 'You tell me,' she shrugged, still with that amazingly calm exterior.

Mandy must have told him exactly what she'd done. She must have worried herself sick afterwards that the silly blind Rachel had gone and done something stupid, like hanged herself or taken a bottle of pills. How novel, she thought. How very dramatic. Poor Mandy, she mused, without an ounce of sympathy, she must have been really alarmed to dare confess to Daniel of all people!

'She's a bitch!' Daniel ground out suddenly, his own thoughts obviously not that far away from Rachel's own. He lurched forward in his chair, hands tightening around the whisky glass. Face clenched too. That tell-tale nerve jumping in his jaw. Elbows pressing into his knees as he glared furiously at the carpet between his spread feet. 'If she hadn't stuck her twisted nose in, you could have been spared all of this! It was over!' he shot out thickly. 'And if she'd only kept her big mouth shut she would have seen it was over! The bitch has always had it in for me. She's been waiting—waiting for me to slip up so she could get her claws into me! But I never thought she'd sink so low as to do it through you!'

That's right, thought Rachel. Blame Mandy. Blame everything and anything so long as it is not yourself.

'Say something, for God's sake!' he ground out, making her blink, because Daniel rarely raised his voice to her like that. And she realised that she had been sitting here just staring blankly at him but not really seeing him. Her eyes felt stuck, fixed in a permanent stare which refused to focus properly—like her emotions—locked on hold until something or someone hit the right button to set them free. She hoped it didn't happen. She had an idea she might fall apart when that happened.

It must feel like this, she pondered flatly, when someone you love dearly dies.

'I want a divorce,' she heard herself say, and was as surprised by the statement as Daniel was, because the idea of divorce hadn't so much as entered her head before she'd said it. 'You can get out. I'll keep the house and the children. You can easily afford to support us.' Another shrug, and she was amazed at her own calmness when she knew she should really be screeching at him like a fishwife.

'Don't be damned stupid!' he ground out. 'That's no damned answer and you know it.'

'Don't shout,' she censured. 'You'll wake the children.'

That seemed to do it, lift the top right off his self-control, and he surged to his feet. The glass was slapped down on the mantel top, whisky slopping over the side to splash on to white marble.

He tried to glare at her but could not hold her steady gaze long enough to gain the upper hand, so he threw himself away instead, his shoulders hunching in the white shirt so that the material became stretched taut across his back, while his hands were thrust angrily into his trouser pockets.

'Look...' he said after a moment, struggling to get hold of himself. 'It wasn't what you think—what that bitch made it out to be! It was just——' he swallowed tensely '—a flash in the pan thing—over before it really began!' He slashed violently at the air with his hand, and Rachel thought, Poor Lydia, guillotined just like that. 'I was under pressure at work. The Harvey take-over was threatening to kill everything I had worked for.' He reached out for his glass of whisky, gulping at the contents like a man with a severe thirst. 'I found I had to work night and day just to keep one step ahead of them. You were still recovering from the bad time you'd had carrying Michael, and I seemed to be spending more time with her than with you. Then the twins got measles—you wouldn't even let me employ a nurse to help you!' he flung at her in accusation. 'So you looked worn out most of the time, and I was worried about you, the sick twins, Michael who refused to sleep more than half an hour at a time, work was getting on top of me and it seemed easier on you if I made myself scarce here, kept my problems confined to the office...' He was talking about a period several months ago when she had believed that everything that could go wrong had gone wrong. She had never so much as considered adding her husband taking up with another woman to her list of problems. It had never entered her head!

'Rachel...' he murmured huskily. 'I never meant to do it. I never even wanted to do it! But she was there when I needed someone and you were not, and I just——'

'Oh—do shut up!'

Nausea hit, and she had to thrust her fist into her mouth to stop herself being sick all over their beautiful Wilton carpet. She crawled to her feet, swaying, sending him a look of hostile warning when he instinctively reached out to steady her, and he flinched away, going grey. She stumbled over to the drinks cabinet and, with her hands shaking violently, poured herself some of his whisky. She hated the stuff, but at that moment felt a dire need to feel its burning vapours shoot through her blood.

He was standing there just watching her, his pose one of violent helplessness as he watched her throw the drink to the back of her throat then stand with her head flung back, eyes closed, while she fought to maintain some control over herself.

But it was all beginning to happen now. Her body was becoming racked by a whole sea of tearing emotions. Her heart was stammering out of rhythm; she wanted to suck in some deep steadying breaths of air but found her lungs unwilling to comply. They were locked up along with the torment. Stomach muscles, ribs, all were paralysed by reaction, while her brain was the opposite, opening up and letting out all the suppressed pain and anguish, letting it taunt her, sniggering and sneering at her until she thought she would pass out.

'It's over, Rachel!' he repeated hoarsely, appealing to her in a voice she had never heard before. 'For God's sake, it's over!'

'And when was it over?' Tipping her head upright, she shrivelled him with a look. 'When my body became yours to indulge yourself in once again? Poor Lydia,' she drawled, the whisky having the desired effect and numbing her from the neck down. 'I wonder which one of us you played for the bigger fool?'

He shook his head, refusing to get into that one. 'It happened,' he stated grimly, raking a shaky hand through his neat dark hair. 'I wish it hadn't, but I can't turn back the clock, no matter how much I want to. If it helps any, I'll admit to feeling utterly ashamed of myself. But as God is my witness,' he added huskily, 'I give you my word that it will never happen again.'

'Until the next time,' she muttered, and was suddenly moving to get out of the room before all the ugly feelings working inside her overflowed in a storm of bitter bile.

'No!' He made a grab for her arm, his fingers biting into her flesh as he pulled her roughly against him, hugging her close while she fought to be free. 'We have to talk this through!' he pleaded thickly. 'Please, I know you're hurting but we need——'

'How many times?' she threw at him, grinding out the words on a complete loss of control. 'How many times did you come home with the scent of her still clinging to your skin? How many times did you have to f-force yourself to make love to me after losing yourself in her!'

'No, no *no*!' he groaned, his arms like steel around her while she struggled angrily to be free. 'No, Rachel! Never! I never let it get that far!' Her huff of scornful disbelief sent him white. 'I love you, Rachel,' he stated hoarsely. 'I love you!'

For some reason that strangled declaration tipped her right over the edge and, on a totally alien burst of violence, she brought her hand up and hit him right across his unfaithful face.

It rocked him—enough to make him let go of her. Rachel stepped back out of reach, her eyes at that moment revealing a murderous kind of hatred that no one who knew her would ever have believed her capable of. And Daniel stood stock-still, digesting the full horror of that look, and was silent.

Without another word she turned and left the room. At the door to their bedroom she paused, then moved away, towards Michael's room.

The child didn't stir when she entered. Rachel walked over to him, leaned gently on the side of the cot and just stared blindly down at her younger son, wondering if the intolerable ache inside her could actually make her physically ill.

Then the dam burst, and on a sob she only just managed to contain while she stumbled over to the single bed which would be Michael's when he grew older, she crawled beneath the Paddington Bear duvet to muffle the sounds of her wretched sobs, sobs which went on and on until she slid into a dark dull sleep.

Morning came with the gurgling of Michael, awake but content at the moment to kick playfully in his cot. And it took Rachel several moments to remember why she was sleeping in his room rather than in her own bed with Daniel.

There was a single crashing feeling inside her as memory returned, then she felt herself go calm again, last night's storm of weeping seeming to have emptied her clean of everything.

She got up, grimacing when she realised she was still wearing the same clothes she'd had on when Mandy called. A hand went to her head, finding the elastic band still partly holding a clump of hair in a tangle of silky knots. She tugged it out then shook her long tresses free. She looked a mess, felt a mess—she hadn't even bothered removing her trainers! She did that now, sitting down on the bed to pull the hot and uncomfortable shoes from her feet just as the baby noticed her and let out a delighted shriek.

She went to bend over his cot, his welcoming smile a balm to her aching heart. And for a while she just immersed herself in enjoying him, tickling his tummy and murmuring all those little nothings mothers shared with their babies, which only babies and mothers understood.

This was hers, she thought wretchedly. No matter what else life wanted to take from her, it could never take away the love of her children.

This, she declared silently, is mine.

He was soaking wet, and she stripped him before attempting to lift him from his cot. Michael was always lively in the mornings, chirping away to himself, bouncing up and down against her while she carried him through to the small bathroom to run the few inches of bath water needed to freshen him up for the day.

She took him, wrapped snugly in a towel, back to his room to dress him. Normally she would then take him downstairs for his breakfast without bothering to get dressed herself. That usually waited until they were all out of the way—at work or at school—but there was no way she could greet the twins looking as she did. They were just too sharp not to wonder out loud why she was still wearing the same clothes she'd had on the night before.

But it took a great gathering together of her courage to enter the room where she knew Daniel would only just be stirring from sleep. She let herself in quietly, searching the gloom for a glimpse of his lean bulk huddled beneath the duvet.

He wasn't there, and it was then that she heard the tell-tale sounds coming from the bathroom. He appeared a moment later, already dressed in a clean white shirt and the trousers of his iron-grey suit. He saw her almost at once and came to an abrupt halt.

In all the years of knowing him, she had never felt so vulnerable in his presence, or so aware of her tumbled appearance: her puffy eyes, made so by too much weeping, her tousled hair hanging limp and untidy around her pale face.

Nor so aware of him: his height, the length of his long, straight body and the tightness of its superbly honed muscles. Wide chest, flat stomach, narrow hips, long powerful legs with...

No. Dry-mouthed, she flicked her gaze warily up to clash with his.

He looked tired, as though he hadn't slept much. He would have been thinking, working things out, trying to find the right solution to an impossible situation. He was good at that—making a success out of a disaster. It was the most fundamental source of his outstanding business success.

His gaze lingered on her face, his own a defensive mask. He had just shaved; his stubborn chin looked clean and shiny-smooth. Rachel caught the familiar scent of his aftershave, and felt her senses stir in response to it. Sexual magnetism held no boundaries, she acknowledged bitterly. Even now, while she was hating and despising him, she was disturbingly aware of him as the man she had loved for so long and so blindly.

Shifting jerkily, she moved over to the bed, lifting a knee on to the soft mattress so that she could lay Michael in the middle. It was only then that she realised that the bed had not been slept in, and the only evidence that Daniel had used it at all was in the imprint of his body on the smooth peach duvet.

Michael was kicking madly, trying to catch his father's attention—attention that was firmly fixed on Rachel. The baby let out a frustrated cry, going red in the face in his effort to pull himself into a sitting position, and Rachel smiled instinctively at his efforts, capturing a waving hand and feeling the instant tug as the child tried to use it for leverage.

Daniel came over to the bed, stretching out to recline on the other side of their son and automatically reaching for the other small hand, which was all Michael needed to lever himself into a sitting position.

'Da!' he said triumphantly, twisting free of both of them so that he could pat his satisfaction on the soft duvet.

Rachel kept her eyes firmly on her son while she felt the searing appeal in Daniel's gaze sting into her pale cheeks. 'Rachel please look at me.' It was a gruff plea that twisted at something wretched inside her, but one she refused to comply with, shaking her head.

'No,' she whispered, keeping her voice level with effort, and Daniel sighed heavily, then reached for Michael, lifting him to kiss the soft baby cheek before placing him further up the bed.

Alerted, Rachel moved to get up, but Daniel was too quick for her, his hand circling her wrist and pulling gently until he had hauled her across the small gap separating them, then enclosing her in the warm strength of his arms.

It's not fair! she thought piteously as her insides dipped and dived with a need to immerse herself in the comfort he was offering her. Her chest became tight, then began to throb with the need to weep, and she let free a constricted gulp in an effort to stop the flood.

'Don't,' he murmured unsteadily.

It had been the wrong thing to say, because the instant he showed her tenderness her control went haywire and she was sobbing deeply into his shoulder. He tightened his arms around her, and lowered his head on to hers. 'Sorry,' he kept saying, over and over. 'Sorry, sorry, sorry...'

But it wasn't enough, was it? It would never be enough. He had killed everything. Love, faith, trust, respect—all gone, and sorry would never bring them back to life again.

'I'm all right now,' she mumbled, making the monumental effort to pull herself together and draw away from him.

But his hold tightened. 'I know I've hurt you unbearably, Rachel,' he murmured, trying to keep a rein on his own distress. She could feel the tension in his chest, in the erratic thump of his heart. 'But don't make any rash decisions while you're in such an...' Emotional state, she guessed he was going to say, but he stopped himself. 'We have everything going for us if you'll just give it another chance. Don't throw it all away because of one stupid mistake on my part. You can't throw it all away!' he insisted thickly.

'I didn't do the throwing away,' she countered, and this time, when she pulled, he let her go, his eyes dark and bleak as he watched her get up from the bed to begin moving around the room searching out fresh clothes, an electric current of suppressed emotion following her as she went from wardrobe to drawers then back again without really being aware of what she was choosing to wear.

All those years of blind trust she had given him, years of quiet understanding and acceptance of his deep personal need to achieve his ambitions. Through all those years she had stayed at home like some pampered pet dog and, so long as he gave her frequent pats of affection, fed the few basic needs she had, like food to eat and water to drink and the occasional trip out in the evening, she had been quite content with her lot.

What a pathetic creature you are! she jeered at herself now. What an utter bore!

Michael let out a wail, and they both started. He wanted his breakfast, and the playful game he had been having with himself had now turned into a demand for some attention.

Rachel stood hovering in the middle of the room, with her clean clothes clutched in her hands while her bemused mind grappled with the problem of what she should do next. Get dressed first or see to Michael first. A simple choice, but she couldn't seem to make it.

It was, in the end, Daniel who lifted the baby into his arms and walked towards the bedroom door. 'I'll see to him,' he said. 'Take your time. It's still quite early.' He let himself out, and Rachel literally sagged beneath the strain of it all.

Breakfast was awful. She seemed intent on flying off the handle at the slightest provocation: from Kate for talking too much, Sam for not putting enough milk on his Weetabix so the biscuits congealed in his dish like two cement bricks which he proceeded to hack at with zeal. She put too much coffee in the filter bag so that it tasted so bitter it was barely drinkable. In the end, angry with herself for over-reacting to everything, frustrated with her inability to cope with her own distraught emotions, she turned on Sam, remembering that he had left his computer out the night before with his selection of games spread all over the floor. By the time she'd finished Sam was stiff and pale, Kate was appalled, Michael silenced and Daniel... Well, Daniel just looked grim. The rest of the morning routine went off in total silence. The children looking openly relieved when Daniel eventually sent them off to their rooms to collect their school things.

'There was absolutely no reason for you to let fly at Sam like that!' Daniel gritted as soon as there was only Michael left to listen. 'You know as well as I do that he's usually the tidiest one of us all! You'll have all three of them a bag of nerves if you don't watch out,' he warned. 'They're good kids. Well-behaved kids for most of the time. I won't let you take it out on them because you're angry with me!'

She whirled on him. 'And since when are you around enough to know how they behave?' she threw at him, seeing to her deep and bitter satisfaction that he stiffened as the thrust went home. 'You see them at breakfast, but only from behind your precious *Financial Times*! You don't even know you have three children most of the time! Y-You love them like you l-love that... Lowry painting you bought—when you remember you've got them, that is. So don't... don't you dare start telling me how to bring up *my* children when as a father you're damned useless!'

What was happening to her? she wondered as she took a jerky step back and Daniel lurched angrily to his feet, glowering at her across the kitchen table and looking fit to hit her. I'm cracking up! she realised dizzily. I'm going to shatter into a million tiny pieces and I don't know if I can stop it!

'You can accuse me of many things, Rachel,' Daniel was murmuring roughly. 'And most of them I probably deserve. But you cannot accuse me of not loving *our* children!'

'Really?' she questioned in sarcastic scorn. 'You only married me in the first place because you got me pregnant with the twins! And even little Michael was a mistake you took your time coming to terms with——!'

His fist slamming down on the table-top stopped her in mid-flow, and her eyelashes flickered nervously as she watched him swing his long body around the table, shifting the heavy pine a good foot off its usual setting when his thigh caught the corner in his haste to reach her. The violence in the air was tangible. Rachel could taste it on her suddenly dry lips as he approached her with his hands outstretched as if he intended throttling her.

As the very last second he changed his mind and grabbed her shoulders instead. It cost him an effort; she could feel him trembling with the need to choke the bitterness right out of her even as he suppressed the urge. 'He's too young to understand the implications of what you've just said,' he rasped out harshly, nodding towards a fascinated Michael. 'But if the twins overheard you, if you've given them any reason at all to think I don't love them, I'll...'

He didn't finish—didn't need to. Rachel knew exactly what he was threatening. He glared at her for a moment longer, then unclipped his hands from her and turned to walk out of the room.

Rachel gulped in a deep breath of air and it was only as she did so that she realised she had stopped breathing altogether. It was pure instinctive need for comfort that made her pick Michael up and cuddle him close.

She felt ashamed of herself, and angry, too, because in lashing out wildly at Daniel like that she had given him the right to attack her when, until that moment, she'd had everything stacked her way.

# CHAPTER THREE

IT WAS the weekend before the twins really began to notice that things weren't quite as they were used to seeing them. And as usual it was the sharp-eyed and more outspoken Kate who wanted to know the reason why.

'Why are you sleeping in Michael's room, Mummy?' she demanded on Sunday morning while they all lingered around the breakfast table, as was their habit on the one day they had to be lazy in the morning.

They had only discovered her new sleeping arrangements because Michael had slept later this morning and, stupidly, Rachel had overslept along with him. Several nights of restless turning in the small bed while her mind tormented her with everything painful and self-pitying it could throw at her had left her exhausted, and last night when she had crawled beneath the Paddington Bear duvet she had achieved—to her relief—an instant blackout, which remained deep and dreamless right up until Sammy came to bounce on her to wake her up.

She still felt haggard, because what the sleep had made up for in hours, it had not made up for in spiritual relief. Wherever her dreams had gone off to last night, they had not eased her aching heart, or her anger, or the waves of bitterness and the soul-crushing self-abhorrence she was experiencing at the way she was letting the whole thing just drag on without doing something about it. Daniel had advised her to make no decisions until she was feeling less emotional and, like the pathetic creature she was, she had used that advice as an excuse to fall into a state of limbo where life had taken on colourless

shapes of muted greys and nothing came into full focus
any more.

Daniel looked no better, the same strain pulling at the
clean-cut lines of his face too. He had been home by six-
thirty every night since their cosy world had exploded
around them. She suspected that the reason for this was
her criticism of him as a father rather than a means to
prove to her that his affair was over. She knew she'd hit
him on the raw there.

So now he came home early enough to take over the
bathing and putting to bed of the children while Rachel
prepared their dinner. And on the surface everything appeared perfectly normal, as they both made an effort to
hide their colossal problems from their children.

Until quietness engulfed the house—then they would
eat their prepared meal in stiff silence, Daniel's few attempts at conversation quashed by her refusal to take
him up on them. So he would disappear into his study
as soon as he possibly could, and she would clear the
remnants of a poorly eaten meal, feed her bleeding
emotions on unreserved bouts of self-pity, then go to
bed in Michael's room, feeling lonelier and more depressed as the days went by.

She was still labouring beneath the weight of a nul-
lifying shock. She could acknowledge that even as she
continued in her zombie-like existence. And Daniel just
watched, grim-faced and silent, waiting, she knew, for
the moment when she would crack wide apart.

Now she had her daughter's curious enquiry to deal
with, and as the truth flooded into her mind and sent
what vestige of colour she had left fleeing from her face,
she managed an acceptable reply. 'Michael is teething
again.'

The corner of Daniel's Sunday paper twitched, and
Rachel knew he was listening, maybe even watching her
over the top of that twitched corner. She didn't glance

his way to find out. She didn't really care what he was doing.

Blonde-haired, blue-eyed, the uncanny image of her mother, Kate nodded understandingly. Michael's teeth had been the scourge of their nights' rest before— although Rachel had not so much as considered swapping beds to be closer to him then. But that did not seem to occur to Kate, who was already turning her attention to her darling daddy.

'I bet you miss having Mummy to cuddle, Daddy,' she remarked, getting down from her chair to go and climb on to Daniel's knee, her long hair flying as she blithely shoved his newspaper aside and made herself comfortable in those big, infinitely secure arms, with the certain knowledge that she was welcome. 'If you'd just told me,' she murmured, with typical Kate guile, 'I would have come and cuddled you instead.'

Tension leaped to life, unspoken words and acid replies flying about the room without being captured.

'That's nice of you, princess.' Daniel folded his paper away so that he could give his adored daughter his full attention. 'But I think I can manage for a little while longer without feeling completely rejected.'

If that last remark had been meant as a message to Rachel, she ignored it, and sat there sipping at her coffee without revealing the effort it cost her to do it.

He was sitting there dressed only in his blue towelling robe, and the cluster of dark hair at his chest curled upwards from between the gaping lapels. He dropped a kiss on his daughter's silky cheek, his smile so openly loving that Rachel felt her stomach tighten then sink, as jealousy, like nothing she had ever experienced before, shot through her, forcing her abruptly to her feet, appalled by what was going on inside her!

Jealous of your own daughter! she castigated herself. How bitter and twisted can you get?

Sheer desperation made her start gathering pots together. Daniel's watchful gaze lifted to her face, and she couldn't stop herself from looking back at him. Something must have shown in the bitter blue glint of her eyes, because his own narrowed speculatively before she spun away and deliberately ruined the relaxed atmosphere by banging around the kitchen, clearing up.

She became even more embittered when her tactics to shift them all didn't work. In fact they simply ignored her as Sam was drawn into conversation with Kate and Daniel, and even Michael, when he insisted on coming out of his high-chair, was promptly placed on Daniel's spare knee where he chattered blithely away to them all in his usual gibberish.

She couldn't stand it. Something in the cosy little scene gnawed into her ragged nerves. She felt left out, alienated by her inability to go over there and join in as she would normally have done. Lydia stood in her way like some huge unscalable wall, blocking her off from her family, from the love and affection she had always taken for granted as her right.

Giving up on clearing up before she broke something, she turned and left the room with a mumbled, 'I'm going to make the beds,' knowing no one heard her, and feeling even more cast out.

She was standing in the middle of their bedroom, just staring blankly into space, when Daniel came in. With a nervy jerk she moved off towards the *en suite* bathroom, trying to look as if that had been where she was making for when he opened the door. When she came out again Daniel was still there, standing at the window with his hands thrust into the deep pockets of his robe. He was big and lean and looked so damned appealing that she wanted to throw something at him— anything to ease this awful ache she was suffering inside.

Forcing herself to ignore him, she began tidying things away. She wanted to make his bed but was now avoiding so much as looking at it while he was present. It had taken on the proportions of a monster since Mandy's call, and each morning she'd had to force herself to come in here to fluff up the pillows and shake out the duvet. It smelled of Daniel—that clean male smell that was uniquely his. It ignited senses she would far rather remained dormant, especially since she wanted to believe he had killed them. But, if anything, her awareness of anything purporting to Daniel seemed to have been intensified rather than dulled. She had found betrayal fed a hateful awareness inside her, and anger fed desire, and pain fed her ability to torment herself with all those feelings she had previously taken for granted.

He turned slightly, watching her in silence as she moved around the room. After a while, when the throbbing silence threatened to choke the very atmosphere in the room, he came to stand in front of her, blocking her path. 'Rachel...' he said gently, willing her to look at him while she was equally determined not to. She looked at the floor between them instead. 'You have remembered I'm in Birmingham all next week?'

No, she had not remembered. But she did so now. Anger at his daring to put his business first, while his private life was in crisis, took the form of ice-cold efficiency. 'What shall I pack?' Was Lydia going? Was it to be a nice cosy double room for two for a week, with no hostile atmosphere to spoil their fun?

Her heart slammed against her breast and she had to fight not to take a step back from him. It would be like conceding some small if obscure point to him to back away, so she stood stiffly, eyes lowered, face a wretched blank.

Physically, it was the closest they'd been to each other since the night the bomb fell on her, and she was tingling all over with that bitter sense of awareness of him.

'Anything,' he dismissed impatiently. She had always packed his case for him when he went off on one of his trips—lovingly folding freshly laundered shirts and carefully counted socks, underwear, handkerchiefs, ties, several suits to wear. And even now, while she silently prayed for him to move out of her way so that she could put a safer distance between them, and her mood wanted to tell him to pack his own bloody case, she was making a mental list of everything he usually required.

Conditioned you are, Rachel! she scoffed at herself. Expertly programmed.

He didn't move, and the tension between them became intolerable. 'Will you be all right?' he asked at last, as though the question was a reluctant one, one he did not want to voice in case she used it as an excuse to attack him. He had been very careful this week to give her nothing which could start the avalanche. 'I...I could get my mother to come and stay if you feel the need for company or——'

'And why should I be in need of company?' She flashed him a bitter look. 'I've managed before when you've been away and I shall manage this time, no doubt, without the need of a baby-sitter.'

He took the taunt about her being one of his helpless children with a tightening of his jaw but without taking her up on it. 'I was not questioning your ability to cope,' he said quietly. 'But you look—tired. And I just wondered if—with everything—you would rather not be on your own right now, that's all.'

Tired, she repeated inside her head. She didn't just look tired, she looked haggard! 'Is your secretary going with you?' Damn, she hadn't meant to ask that question.

In fact, she had been determined not to so much as breathe it!

'Yes, but——'

'Then I won't have to concern myself about your comfort, will I?'

'Rachel,' he sighed, 'Lydia isn't——'

'I don't want to know.' She pushed by him, preferring to let her body brush against his than to stand here any longer enduring this kind of conversation.

'Why did you ask the damned question, then?' he barked, then made a concerted effort to control himself again. 'Rachel, we *have* to talk about this!'

She was making the bed now, gritting her teeth and getting on with the job because it was the only thing left in the room to do.

'It can't go on any longer.' He appealed for common sense. 'You must see that! Kate has noticed, which means she'll be on the alert from now on, watching, calculating how long you stay in Michael's room when——'

'And we must not upset your darling Kate, must we?' she flashed, then almost cried out in horror at herself. How could she be feeling jealous of her own child! Blindly, horribly jealous of that poor sweet child who possessed her father's love by right!

'Uncalled for, Rachel,' Daniel grimly rebuked, and she agreed, sickeningly so.

The bed was made. Now she could get out of...

'Let me just explain about Lydia,' Daniel said carefully. 'She isn't——'

'Are you planning on being here for the rest of the day?'

That threw him. It shut him up about his precious Lydia, too. 'Yes.' He frowned in puzzlement. 'Why?'

'Because I want to go out, and if you're here it saves me having to ask your mother to come and mind the children.' Why she had said that, Rachel had no idea.

It had not been a conscious decision to go anywhere. But, once said, she found the idea of being on her own for a while—completely on her own—something that was suddenly vital to her sanity.

She made a dive for the wardrobe, trembling in her sudden urgency to get out of the house and away from them all. She dragged out the first thing that came to hand—her rainproof anorak. Daniel seemed momentarily stunned, and just stood there staring at her for the time it took her to shrug the coat on.

Then he sprang to life. 'If you want to go out somewhere, Rachel, you only had to say so!'

The zip was being stubborn and she stood, head bent, grappling with it. It was so hot in here today! Struggling with the zip was making her hot. Was it possible to suffocate in one's emotions? she wondered frantically. Because that was what she felt she was doing. People closing her in, walls... feelings.

'Give me ten minutes while I get dressed myself, then we'll all go out together...'

Shoes! She hadn't put on any shoes! On another jerk, she was crouching on the floor and scrabbling around in the bottom of her wardrobe while Daniel seemed glued to the spot in stunned confusion.

She found her black leather boots and sat down on the carpet to pull them on, tucking the bottoms of her narrow jeans inside with fingers that shook.

'Rachel... don't do this!' It must have hit him then that she really meant to go out alone because his voice was rough and urgent. 'You've never gone out without us before,' he rasped. 'Wait until we can all...'

She was vaguely listening to him, though only from behind a wall of dark self-absorption. But one small part of what he had said got through. Daniel was right, and she never did go anywhere without one or all of them accompanying her! If it wasn't Daniel, then it was the children—or his mother! All her adult life she had lived beneath the protective wing of others. Her parents first, her more outward-going friends, Daniel! Mostly Daniel.

She was almost twenty-five years old, for God's sake! And here she was, a dowdy little housewife with three children and a husband who...

'I'm going alone!' she raked at him. 'It won't hurt you to have the children to yourself for once!'

'I never said it would!' he sighed impatiently. 'But Rachel, you've never——'

'Exactly!' Jumping up she spun away from him when he made a grab for her, concern raking at his taut face. 'While you've been busy making your fortune, chasing your personal rainbows and having your affairs,' she threw at him bitterly, 'I've been quietly sitting here in this damned house—stagnating!'

'Don't be stupid!' He made another lunge for her wrist and caught it this time. 'This is ridiculous. You're behaving like a child! It——'

'But that's just it, Daniel, don't you see?' she cried, appealing for his understanding even while rebellion ran crazily through her veins. 'That is exactly what I am— a child! A very spoiled, very overprotected child! I never grew up because I've never been given the chance to grow up! I was seventeen when I married you!' she choked out wretchedly. 'Still at school! And, before you came along, my parents used to wrap me in cotton wool! My God, what a shock it must have been to them when they discovered their sweet little innocent daughter had been sleeping with the big bad wolf without them knowing it!'

He laughed; she knew he couldn't help it because her description of himself was so damned accurate that it was either laugh or weep.

'So, I get pregnant,' she went on tightly, 'and swap one set of parents for another set—you and your mother!'

'Now that's not true, Rachel,' Daniel protested. 'I've never looked on you as a child. I——'

'Liar!' she declared. 'You damned hypocritical liar! And you know what makes you a liar, Daniel?' she demanded shrilly. 'It's the way you're beginning to panic because I want to spend some time on my own—because it could be Kate making the demand by the way you're reacting!'

'This is crazy!' he breathed, shaking his dark head as though he couldn't believe this conversation was taking place.

'Crazy?' she repeated. 'You think it's crazy? Well, how the hell do you think I feel knowing that I let you do this to me? I actually sat back and let you treat me like this—and look where it's got me! I've ended up a twenty-four-year-old has-been with three children and a husband who's already bored out of his mind with me! Oh, please let me go!'

On a wretched sob she twisted herself free, and made for the door. And it was with the walls around her looking strangely topsy-turvy that she stumbled down the stairs and through the front door, only just aware enough of what she was doing to remember to snatch up her purse from the hall table as she flew past it.

Her white Escort was blocked in by Daniel's black BMW so she simply ran off down the drive, away from the smart modern detached house that had been brand-new when they moved into it five years ago, one of a set built on a small but exclusive estate in one of London's executive belts. A house she had loved from the moment she walked into it because it offered them all so much more space after the tiny inner-city terraced house they had rented before.

Now she wanted only to get as far away from it as she could, and she hurried down the quiet tree-lined street and on to the main road, aware that Daniel would not come after her. It would take him ages to dress himself and three children before he could bundle them in the car to come looking for her. But knowing that did not stop her jumping on the first bus which came along.

Central London it was making for, so central London was where she was going to go. She sat staring miserably out of the bus window, where dust and grime and dried raindrops formed unsightly patterns across her vision. She could just make out the park where she often took the children to play—or was it they who took her? She didn't know any more. She didn't feel as if she knew anything for a certainty any more.

Collar turned up against the cool, late September air, hands stuffed into her pockets, blond head lowered, she walked the Sunday-quiet streets of London, lost inside a great pitiless sea of misery, her feelings becoming more battered as that cruel inner eye opened wider and wider to give her a ruthlessly honest look at who the real Rachel Masterson was.

She was a twenty-four-year-old woman who had become emotionally stuck at the age of seventeen, she decided. She, in her fantasy-like existence, had believed Daniel loved her because he made love to her, and she had never once questioned that love.

But she did now. And, though it galled her to do it, she found he had to be admired for the way he had calmly accepted responsibility when she became pregnant.

Daniel had simply paid his dues for getting himself involved with a young innocent. And if he did lead a separate life outside the one he shared with her, then maybe he considered that his due.

And a separate life it was, she accepted grimly. For it was only now, as she felt her cosy world rocking precariously on the very axis which supported it, that she realised that he hadn't ever drawn her into sharing with him that faster, more exciting life he led beyond the confines of his neat, well-ordered marriage. A marriage he had created for her to play at being housewife and mother to his children because it was what she'd wanted to do.

Did she only play? She didn't even know that any more.

Hours she walked, hours and hours without noticing them drift by. Hours just thinking, hurting, fielding the wretchedness of her own misery, until sheer exhaustion turned her feet towards home.

She caught a taxi, because she was tired, and because she was cold, and because home was suddenly the one place in the world she most wanted to be.

Which left her feeling somewhat defeated, because it also meant that her short grasp for freedom had done her no good at all.

# CHAPTER FOUR

DANIEL was sprawled out on the sitting-room sofa when she entered the room. He had a book thrust in front of his face and was giving a good impression of someone who had not shifted his position in hours. He made no effort to acknowledge her, and after a short pause while she waited in defiance for the expected explosion which never came, she shut the door and went into the kitchen. She was smiling to herself as she went though, because he hadn't fooled her for a moment with that air of indifference—she had seen the sitting-room curtain twitch as she paid the cabby. For some reason his need to hide his concern put a lighter step in her walk.

The coffee dripped through its filter into the jug and Rachel watched it absently. Her coat was thrown across the back of one of the kitchen chairs, her boots standing neatly by the door.

He entered like a cat stalking its prey on silent tread, shoeless, his casual trousers a snug fit to his flat hips, his dark green fleeced cotton shirt tucked loosely into them.

'You'd better call Mandy,' he muttered, kicking out a chair and dropping into it.

'Why?' Rachel glanced at him and then away again, her tone lacking a single spark of interest in his reply.

'Because I've been giving her hell all day, believing you were there and she wasn't telling me.'

'And how do you know for sure it wasn't exactly like that?'

There was a pause before he said reluctantly, 'Because I got my mother to watch the children and went round to her flat to see for myself.'

'So now both your mother and Mandy know I escaped for the day,' she noted drily. The coffee was ready, and she lifted a pretty painted mug down from the rack.

'You can't blame me for worrying about you when you went off half-cocked like that,' he grunted, looking uncomfortable.

Good! she thought. That should teach him not to treat me like a child. I might be one, but it doesn't mean I want to be treated like one. And, anyway, it might do him some good to realise that his predictable little wife is not so predictable after all.

She sat down opposite him, hugging the hot mug in her hands because they still felt cold. Daniel slouched in his chair, his forearms resting on the table and his fingers twining tensely as though he was struggling with something uncomfortable inside. His head was bent, his hair untidy—as though he had spent the day raking his fingers through the thick black mass.

She had never seen him like this before, lacking his usual poise.

'Your parents know too,' he said suddenly. 'I rang them when I couldn't think of anywhere else you could have gone. They've been expecting you to turn up in Altrincham all afternoon. You'd better give them a ring to let them know you're OK.'

So, it needed just three places to check before he ran out of ideas where to look for her. What did that tell her about herself? Having done enough self-analysis for one day, she decided to put that one in abeyance for the time being.

'I'll tell you what, Daniel,' she suggested instead. 'Why don't *you* call them back, since it was you who worried them all in the first place? Call your mother—and Mandy too while you're at it. I have no wish to speak to her personally,' she added coolly.

'Who—my mother?' He sounded startled.

'Mandy,' she drawled sarcastically, surprised, because he had to be feeling knocked off balance a bit to make that kind of mistake. Daniel was not usually stupid. 'You brought her back into this mess after making much of her learning to mind her own business, so you call her back, if you think she's that bothered.'

'We were all bothered!' he snapped, sweeping her an angry glance.

'I'm not suicidal, you know,' she informed him levelly, sipping at her coffee and feeling more at ease the more tense he became. 'I might have been a dumb-brained fool where you're concerned, but I won't be forfeiting the rest of my life because of it.'

'I never so much as considered you were!' he grunted, adding gruffly, 'I never considered you dumb-brained either.'

'Of course you did,' she argued. 'When you bothered wasting valuable time considering me at all, that is,' she added witheringly.

He sucked in a short breath, fighting not to rise to the bait. 'Where did you go?' he asked.

'To London,' she told him, bringing his head up sharply.

'Where in London?' he demanded. 'Doing what? You've been out since ten o'clock this morning. That's almost twelve hours! What the hell did you find to do in London with all the stores closed that could take twelve bloody hours?'

'Maybe I found myself a man!' she taunted, watching with a mild fascination as his face drained of all colour. 'It isn't that difficult to pick one up, you know.' She twisted the knife while he was still off balance from her first stab at him. 'Maybe I decided to take a leaf out of

your book and go in search of some—comfort, because
the going at home suddenly got tough!'

He shot to his feet, knocking the chair to the ground
with a clatter. 'Stop it!' he rasped, raking a hand through
his tousled hair. 'Stop trying to score points off me,
Rachel! It isn't like you to take pleasure in hurting
others.'

No, it wasn't, she agreed. Funny really, how one's
nature could alter virtually overnight. Whereas once she
would never have dreamed of striking out at anyone, she
was suddenly consumed with the desire to cut to the raw!
She didn't even care that her parents would be worrying
about her. Or that Daniel's mother was probably sitting
in her flat not a mile away from here on tenterhooks,
waiting to hear that her darling Rachel had returned
safely to the fold.

'Then go and make your phone calls,' she advised,
returning her attention to the drink in her hands. 'Then
you won't have to listen, will you?'

He glared at her across the length of the kitchen table,
looking ready to reach across and shake her if she pro-
voked him so much as an inch further. Then, surprisingly, he sighed harshly and turned and walked out of
the room. She heard his study door close with a suppressed violence and grimaced to herself.

She went upstairs to use the bathroom while he was
busy on the telephone, stuffing her long hair into a
shower-cap and taking a quick shower, only then remembering, as she was hurriedly tying her fluffy long
white bathrobe around her so that she could get out of
the bedroom before he came up, that she had not packed
his case.

On a silent curse she hurried into the bedroom, to dig
out his soft black leather all-purpose suit-bag, and laid
it on the bed to unbuckle the straps.

'You don't need to do that,' his tight voice informed her from the bedroom doorway. 'I cancelled this afternoon.'

'Oh, dear,' she drawled as he closed the bedroom door. 'Lydia will be disappointed.'

*That's it*! he might as well have shouted, the way his lean body jerked as though someone had cracked a whip at him. Rachel knew a moment's real panic as she stared into his face, white with angry frustration, then was given no opportunity to do anything other than gasp as he reached her in two strides and dragged her against him.

'I can't take any more of this,' he muttered. 'Nothing I can say or do is going to change your mind about me!'

'But I *have* changed my mind about you!' she countered, afraid of the hectic glitter she could see burning in his eyes, but refusing to show it. 'I used to think you were a saint, but now I know you're a bastard!'

'Then a bastard I will be!' he snarled, and dropped his mouth down on to hers.

He used no persuasion, no gentle coaxing to get what he wanted from her, but just forced her tight lips apart by sheer brute force. She groaned in protest, his fingers like clamps on her aching shoulders, holding her up to him while the rest of her body curved frantically away from him in an effort not to come into full contact with his traitorous frame.

His tongue snaked into her mouth and she tried to bite down on it, but he was expecting it, and just increased the pressure against her lips until they were pressed hard back against her teeth, then slid his tongue sensually over hers. She shuddered, her hands closing into fists that she pushed into his muscled ribcage in a hopeless attempt to try to stem the unbidden firing in her blood which told her she was vulnerable to him; even though she hated him to the very depths of her being, she was still vulnerable to this.

Another groan, and she kicked out at him with a bare
foot. It made no difference. He was not going to release
her, and her straining body was simply a supple wand
he bent to his will. Taking one hand off her shoulder to
loop it around her slender waist, he moved the other to
her hair, winding the long silken swath around his fingers
in a tight coil before he tugged cruelly to keep her mouth
turned up to receive his kiss.

She was burning up inside her thick towelling robe,
her body stinging with a prickly heat that made it all the
more sensitive to the hard body now clamped tightly
against her. And it wasn't just her temperature that had
gone haywire, it was her senses—her senses firing out
of control, wanting this, swarming towards it like bees
to the sweetest honey ever made on this earth.

It's not fair! she thought wretchedly, it's just not fair
that he can still do this to me! She hated herself—and
despised him for making her acknowledge her own
weakness.

'Damn you!' she cursed, when at last he came up for
air. His cheeks were flushed, his eyes dark pools of bitter
frustration as they glared down at her.

'Yes,' he agreed on a raw, driven hiss. 'Damn me to
hell! But you want me, Rachel. You want me so badly
that you're literally choking on it. So what does that
make you in this nightmare?'

She flinched, the full bitter truth in his cruel taunt
making something she had been holding on to for days
now snap inside her—she actually felt it give, and she
leaned back against his constricting arm, careless of the
painful pull it placed on her scalp, careless of everything
now as, with an animal growl that was as alien to her
as it was to the man who was goading her, she went for
him with her nails.

Good reflexes saved his face from serious damage. His
head snapped back out of harm's way just in time, and

her nails only managed to graze his neck from jawbone to the open collar of his shirt.

'You little cat!' he choked, long strands of strong silken hair clinging to his fingers when he released her to put his hand to his scratched neck.

'I hate you!'

'Good,' he grunted, and he pulled her back against him. 'That will make it easier when I take you, when the method of taking will make no difference to how you feel about me.'

'That's right!' she jeered. 'Why not add rape to adultery?'

'Rape?' he derided harshly. 'Since when did I ever have to resort to rape with you?' His tone sent shivers of self-revulsion rushing through her. 'In all my life I've never known a more sexually eager woman than you!'

'What—even Lydia?'

She was thrust unceremoniously away from him, his arms raking a wide, defeated arc before both hands went up to grip his nape as if he had to hold on to something or hit her. And he stared at her with something close to torment burning in his eyes. 'Stop it, Rachel,' he whispered thickly. 'Stop trying to rile me into doing something we'll both regret!'

Was that what she was doing? Riling him like some she-devil, wanting him to take her in anger—to prove to her totally that he was all the rotten things she was thinking about him?

Yes, she realised, that was exactly what she was doing as she continued to stand there, goading him with the hot glitter of her eyes when really she should be getting out of here while the chance to escape was good. She wanted to feed the hatred she felt towards him—the anguish, the bitter disappointment she was feeling, and last of all the great lump of pain that had not shifted from the centre of her chest since Mandy called.

And she heard herself, as if from the other end of a long dark tunnel, goad him further. 'Then get out!' she told him shrilly. 'Why don't you just do the honourable thing, Daniel, and get the hell out of here! No one's making you stay! There's nothing left here to stop you going to your precious Lydia!'

'Will you stop mentioning her bloody name?' he grated.

'Lydia,' she chanted instantly. 'Lydia—Lydia—*Lydia*!'

Something flared in his eyes—anguish?—gone before it could be proved. Then he was reaching for her again, top lip curling bitterly as he pulled her hard against him.

'No,' he muttered. 'You—you—*you*!'

And in a single swift movement he had turned them both and tipped them off balance so that they landed in a tangle of limbs on the bed behind them.

What followed was less loving than anything could be. It was a battle. A battle to see who could arouse whom more. A battle of the senses where each deliberate caress was answered by a matching one, each clash of their hot angry eyes taunted—scorned. The more aroused the one became, the more the other fed it, driving each other on some crazy helter-skelter ride of pained, fractured emotions.

There was a moment within it all when Daniel seemed to make a flailing grab for sanity, snatching at his self-control and making to move away from her. But Rachel saw it coming, and on a flash of blinding panic which seemed to have its roots in a terrible fear of losing him altogether, she reached for him, her mouth finding his with an urgency that made him groan out her name in a wretched plea against her marauding lips. But she took no notice. And it was suddenly Rachel playing the seducer, Rachel conducting things from desperate beginning to wild tumultuous end, leaving the man beneath her shaken and spent while she could only crawl away to huddle in a ball of miserable frustration, her senses clawing for a release they had been denied. And she felt appalled, disgusted with herself.

So who won the battle? she asked herself bleakly. Neither had won, she concluded. She just felt sickened by her own wanton behaviour and the knowledge that she had been driven to it by a fear of losing him—no matter what he had done—and another driving need to feel him lose himself completely in her. It had been essential—essential to her sanity to know that, no matter how many Lydias there had been for him, she, little boring Rachel, could still turn him inside out with desire for her.

And, she had to acknowledge finally, she had wanted him, wanted him with a need which had left no room for pride or self-respect. But in the end even that had not been enough to help her find at least some release from the pressures that had been culminating inside her over the last terrible week. It was as though her wounded soul refused to let her give him that final conquest. Would it ever again?

A single tear slid out from the corner of each staring eye and ran their slow meandering way down her pale cheeks. She, in her twisted need to prove some obscure point to herself, had lost in the end, because what she had gained in discovering she could still rock him she had lost in her own failure to respond. Her blind trust in him had gone, and taken with it her right to love and respond freely.

It hurt, it frightened her, and it left her feeling more lonely than she could have felt if he'd just walked out and left her. Because she didn't know how she was ever going to be any different with him now.

'Rachel?' She turned her head on the pillow to find him watching her, his eyes two dark and sombre points in the darkness. 'I'm sorry,' he said quietly.

Sorry for failing her just now in this bed? she wondered. Or sorry for the whole damned blasted mess in its entirety? In the end, she decided, it didn't really matter. Nothing seemed to matter any more. She was an empty husk, lost and alone, and no amount of sorrys was ever going to make her feel any better.

The tears glazed her eyes again, seeping in a wretched spill on to her lashes. 'I'm ashamed of myself,' she told him, in a voice thick and quivering.

Something suspiciously like moisture swam across his eyes and his answering sigh was decidedly shaky. 'Come here,' he said, and reached out to pull her to him. His arms enfolded her, his body drawing into a curve which almost totally cocooned her. 'On the vow of a man who has never felt so wretched in his life, Rachel,' he murmured into the tangled silk of her hair, 'I swear I will never do anything that could hurt you like this again.'

Could she afford to believe him? she wondered bleakly. It would be easy enough to let herself believe him. Forgive and forget and shove it all to the back of her mind in the hope that it would take the hurt with it.

'I love you,' he told her huskily. 'I do love you, Rachel.'

'No!' She stiffened violently at that, all thoughts of forgiving gone with the utterance of those three false words. She had believed them once before and look where it had got her! 'Don't speak of love to me,' she choked out angrily. 'Love had nothing to do with what happened just now—or why you married me at all for that matter!'

Breakfast the next morning was an awkward affair. The twins kept sending her glances which were both troubled and curious. She knew they must be wondering about her sudden disappearance yesterday, but it was obvious they were under orders from Daniel not to question her.

She even allowed herself a small smile when Kate opened her mouth to ask something, only to close it again with a mutinous snap at the warning look Daniel sent her. Sam was different. He kept frowning at her but otherwise said nothing, and that was the worry—he hadn't spoken a single word since coming down to breakfast.

'Eat up, Sammy,' Rachel said gently to him after watching him toy with his Weetabix for long enough. 'You'll be complaining of being hungry by mid-morning if you don't.'

Those eyes beneath their frowning brows, so like his father's, glanced at her. 'Where did you go yesterday!' he burst out suddenly, sending a wary look towards his father's pink newspaper.

Rachel glanced at it too. 'I—took the day off,' she answered lightly, smiling at him to show him everything was all right. 'You didn't mind, did you?'

He shifted uncomfortably, and Rachel felt her heart squeeze for him. He wasn't like his irrepressible twin, who did her worrying all up front. Sammy did it all within himself, and for him to speak out like this meant he had to be really bothered about her sudden out-of-character move. 'But—where did you go?' he persisted.

Rachel sighed inwardly, instinctively reaching across the table to comb her fingers through his ruthlessly flattened-down hair. He did not jerk away or protest at her messing him about, as he would usually have done.

'I was—tired,' she explained, floundering in her effort to offer a reason fit for a six-year-old to understand. 'Feeling—all shut-in and restless. So I went out on my own for a while, that's all.'

'But you aren't used to going out without one of us to look after you!' he said, glaring at the lowering pink paper, almost warning his father to stay out of this.

'Who says?' she teased, trying to make a joke of it when in actual fact she was appalled to realise that even her six-year-old son thought her incapable of looking after herself! 'I am all grown-up, you know. And quite capable of looking after myself.'

'But Daddy said you weren't,' chipped in Kate. 'He told Grandma. He stormed around the house. Up and down, in and out.' As blithe as can be, Kate spoke about the forbidden and brought the newspaper all the way down. 'And he kept on shouting down the phone at Aunty Mandy.'

'That's enough, Kate,' Daniel said quietly, but his tone was enough to bring those wide innocent eyes around to his in surprise.

'But you did!' she insisted. 'You were behaving like a—a mad bull!'

'A what?' Daniel choked.

'A mad bull,' she repeated poutingly. 'That's what my teacher calls us when we charge around all over the place. "Mad bulls belong in fields," she says.' Kate gave a very good impression of her teacher's firm voice. 'Well, you charged around here yesterday, didn't you? And see——' she smiled one of her deliberately beguiling smiles, usually guaranteed to have her father eating out of her hand '—Mummy came back all safe and sound, just like I said she would!'

So at least one of her family thought her capable of looking after herself! Thanks, Kate, Rachel thought drily. 'Eat your breakfast,' was what she actually said. 'As you all can see, I returned safe and sound, so let's forget it, shall we?'

'You can go to Birmingham if you want to,' she told Daniel as soon as the children went off to collect their school things.

He was checking his briefcase, folding away his newspaper and placing it inside when she spoke. He paused, his long fingers stilling on the leather lid, then continued to close and lock the case.

He looked every bit the successful businessman this morning in his crisp white shirt and charcoal suit—suddenly very out of place in this homely kitchen with its mad clutter of family living. He would look just perfect in the breakfast-room of an elegant Georgian manor house, surrounded by rich mahogany furniture with the weak morning sunlight spilling in through a deep bay window. And it hit her suddenly that, while she had been standing still for the last seven years, Daniel had been growing further and further away.

'It's no longer necessary for me to go.' He declined her offer coolly. 'Jack Brice can handle things as well as I could.'

Then why wasn't he going in the first place? she wanted to ask, but didn't because the answer could only hinge upon Lydia.

'Are you worried that I might walk out on you if you do go?' she asked, with a genuine interest in his reply. Daniel cared for her and the children, she knew, but would it be that much of a tragedy if they were no longer a part of his life?

He spun away to go and stand by the kitchen window that overlooked the toy-cluttered rear garden, his hands lost in his trouser pockets. 'Yes,' he admitted grimly at last.

And Rachel was shocked by the overwhelming sense of relief she experienced at his answer—which in turn made her angry, because it only exposed her own weakness. 'It isn't my place to leave,' she pointed out. 'You must know that prerogative is all yours.'

'Yes.' His dark head dipped for a moment before he turned back to the table. He didn't look at her, but made a play of checking his briefcase again. 'I know that if I had a self-respecting bone left in my body, I would be shifting my stuff out of here and leaving you with some semblance of pride intact. But I don't want to leave. I don't want to break up what we have—had,' he corrected grimly. 'I know I have to prove myself to you again. I know it's going to take time. But I won't give in, Rachel.' He looked at her at last, his eyes dark and determined. 'You can throw what the hell you like at me, but it won't be me who will do the walking.'

'I could slap a separation order on you,' she hit out at him suddenly, aware that she was only doing it to hide her own weak fears. 'Make you move out.'

Daniel frowned at her. 'How the hell could you know about things like that?' he demanded. He was wondering if she had already taken legal advice from somewhere. He didn't really think her capable of it, but he wasn't sure.

She liked to see him looking uncertain. It lifted her ego, so she just shrugged indifferently and said with heavy sarcasm, 'I watch a lot of TV.'

'And are you going to?' he asked. 'Begin the end of our marriage?'

He was clever; she had to give it him. With one blunt question he had neatly dropped the responsibility into her lap. 'You began the deterioration of this marriage, Daniel,' she threw back levelly. 'But—no,' she answered his question. 'I'm not intending doing anything about the situation—just yet.'

'Then why not now?' he sighed out wearily, unhooking his jacket from the back of the chair and shrugging it on. Rachel watched him, saw the flash of gold on his left hand, put there all those millions of years ago. It was nothing but a slender band of gold, very plain, very cheap. They had not been able to afford anything better. She had a matching one of her own—and an engagement ring bought for her several years after they were married and finances were beginning to get a little easier. It was just a single diamond solitaire, small but neat on her slender finger.

He had told her he loved her then, she recalled. 'I love you, Rachel,' he'd said as he slid the little ring on her finger. 'Without you and the twins, all the hard work would have no meaning.'

But he was wrong. Without them, Daniel would be twice the success he was today; she was sure of it.

He was studying her now with that shuttered look while he waited for her to answer his question. She found his eyes, and held on to them for a moment before dropping her gaze to her cup. 'I don't know,' she answered honestly. 'But I think I want to see you bleed.'

Surprisingly, he smiled, a hand going to his neck where the evidence of her attack last night just showed above the collar of his shirt. 'I thought you'd already done that,' he said ruefully.

'Not enough,' she said, flushing slightly despite her determination not to apologise for that particular attack.

'Ah,' he said.

'Yes,' she agreed. 'Ah.'

'So I am about to enter a period of—retribution.' He smiled again, then bent to drop a kiss on top of Michael's golden head. 'So be it,' he said, and strode arrogantly from the room, leaving Rachel feeling ever so slightly—flattened.

But, oddly, it didn't quite work like that. Instead of meeting him with a cold face and a biting tongue, she found herself avoiding anything that could even hint at trouble. And over the next few weeks they seemed to slip into a weird kind of limbo, as though their marriage had fallen into a coma—a period where they were being given time to recover a little before having to face the future for what it was to be.

She did not go back to sleeping in Michael's room. But she didn't know why she went back to sleeping with Daniel. Neither did she refuse him when he would reach for her in the dark silences their nights had become. But even though they shared a kind of loving, it never quite managed to reach any real level of satisfaction for either of them, she guessed. She would go with him, move with him, and travel that long sensual path towards fulfilment—want to travel it! But suddenly she would see herself in her mind's eye, entwined and pulsing with desire in his arms, feel his body trembling against her own, his breath just soft gasps of sensual urgency against her sensitised flesh—then see Lydia in her place, Lydia in his arms, Lydia driving him to the same state of mindless passion. And she would pull frantically away from him, halting their loving as effectively as switching off the power that drove them.

Then she would lie, curled up and away from him, shivering her distress in lonely torment while Daniel would lie beside her, an arm covering his face, knowing, even though they never spoke about it—never tried to resume making love—that Lydia had come between them as surely as if she'd crawled into the bed with them. The hurt and betrayal, the cruel twist of jealousy would all rush back to flay her, and Rachel could not bear him so much as to touch her. And Daniel never tried.

She spent her days worrying about it, frightened because she knew that if anything was likely to send him back into Lydia's arms, then it was surely her stupid if unintentional hot and cold tactics.

That Daniel saw this as the form her retribution was to take only made her feel worse, because retribution was the very last thing on her mind when he would reach for her in the night.

And knowing this only made her more tense, more aware of how her own self-respect suffered every time she let him try to love her, because she knew she should be scorning him even before it started. Yet she needed him, even while her ability to respond was sadly retarded, she needed what small amount of succour she could glean from his loving—and she needed to know that Daniel needed her.

# CHAPTER FIVE

DANIEL'S mother began spending more time with her during the day. She never mentioned the Sunday Rachel had escaped, but it was always there in the careful guard she kept on her expression, in the stealthy way she trod around certain subjects.

Jenny Masterson was proud of her son. He had dragged himself up from lean beginnings, made a success of his career when all the advantages had been stacked against him. But she wasn't blind to what temptation could be put in the way of a man of Daniel's calibre. He was quick, shrewd, and clever. He was nearly thirty-two years old and already a respected member of the business community. The whiz-kid who had to be watched.

Star quality, with the looks to go with the label.

Women had to be interested in him because those dark good looks and his ability to make money out of nothing made him interesting to them. And, although nothing had been said to her as to why her son's marriage was suddenly very rocky, Jenny was no fool, and most probably had had a fairly accurate idea of the truth. So she spent more time with Rachel, offering moral support in her quiet solid way, and Rachel was grateful, for she had also come to the bleak realisation that Jenny was her only friend in this new alien world she was living in right now.

Which in turn made her feel restless, utterly dissatisfied with herself and the empty person she had allowed herself to become. Her home, which had once been her pride and joy, now became a place to see criticism in every corner. It was good enough for her, but not for Daniel. His advancement in life meant he deserved something grander—something which would reflect the successful man he had become. And she would flay herself by remembering all those times when he had tried to talk her into moving into something bigger, better, and, with this new way she had developed of looking at him, she began to understand why. No wonder he never brought any of his business colleagues home with him—he was most probably ashamed of the place!

Then, contrarily, she would be angry with him for not letting her into that other world he moved in. She might be guilty of being a silly blind fool who had barely changed in seven long years, but he had helped keep her that way by hiding her away like some guilty secret that did not fit his smart successful image!

Anger became resentment, and resentment a restlessness that made her quick-tempered and irritable—unpredictable to the point where she knew those around her trod warily, yet she couldn't seem to do anything about it.

What are you, Rachel? she asked herself one evening when—as had been perhaps inevitable after weeks of being home on the dot of six-thirty—Daniel was working late, and the restlessness grew worse because he wasn't there and she wanted him to be—needed him to be to feel any kind of peace with herself.

You can't blame Daniel for everything that has gone wrong, she told herself. You've been existing in oblivion. So wrapped up in your own cosy little world that you didn't even bother to wonder about the one he moves in beyond your sphere! You knew he went to business dinners a lot. You knew he had to move in certain circles if he was to keep his ear to the ground, but you never once wondered whether you should be moving there with him, listening with him—helping and supporting him!

You didn't even know the Harvey take-over had been wrapped up until Mandy told you! And the only reason you knew there *was* a thing called a Harvey take-over was because Daniel's mother had risen in his defence one night when you were bickering on about never seeing him. 'He's tied up with this Harvey take-over!' she'd said. 'Don't you realise how important it is that he wins this one?'

No, she hadn't, and no, she still didn't, because she had never bothered trying to find out! What did that make her in this marriage between two people that was nothing more than a house and a bed and three children they shared?

'I'm not even beautiful!' she sighed into the mirror one morning. Not in the classical sense of the word anyway. My figure is OK, I suppose, when you take into account that I've had three children. And my legs aren't that bad. But my face wouldn't stop traffic. It isn't the kind of face you would expect to see on the wife of a man like Daniel Masterson, is it? My eyes are too big, nose too small, mouth all cute and vulnerable-looking.

She scowled at her reflection in distaste.

And just look at my hair! she thought, lifting it up so that the long twisting strands fanned out on a crackle of golden static. I've been wearing my hair like this since I was Kate's age!

'Talk about Peter Pan!' she muttered in disgust. 'He has nothing on me!—even my choice of clothes is utterly juvenile!'

Then do something about it, an impatient-sounding voice inside her head challenged.

Why not? she mused, on a sudden new surge of restless defiance.

'I tell you what, Mike,' she turned to say to the baby playing happily on the bedroom carpet, 'I'm going shopping for a whole new wardrobe of clothes! We'll see if Grandma will come and look after you. And if she won't, well—' her full bottom lip took on a mulish pout, just as Kate's did when set on some determined course '—we'll just go and dump you on your papa for the day—and let him stew in that for a change!'

But Daniel's mother was quite happy to mind the baby, which took the wind out of Rachel's sails somewhat. She'd quite liked the idea of marching into Daniel's ultra-modern office building and dumping his youngest child into his stunned arms! Mind you, she pondered as the taxi took her to London, it was one thing imagining herself doing something like that, but it was quite another actually carrying it out.

Underneath the defiance the timid Rachel still huddled, happy being just what she was and wishing she could stay like that.

And was it so wrong to be completely lacking in any personal ambition except to want to be a good wife and mother? she then demanded angrily of herself. She'd always loved her job. Loved being there for her children, having time to listen to them, play with them, or simply just enjoy them!

And Daniel. Daniel might stride like a lion through the cut-throat jungle of big business, but she knew how the tension would drain from his face and body when he came home to his ordinary family with their ordinary problems, waiting for him to sort them out.

He might come in through their front door at night looking grim and remote—wearing the face of a ruthless hunter, she realised now with clearer insight into the man himself—but within half an hour he would be stretched out on the floor with the twins, playing some really or-dinary board game, or sitting cross-legged between the

two in front of the television set, his mental processes
dropped right down to their level while they battled
against each other at one of Sammy's computer games—
and there wouldn't be a sign of grimness or tension in
him, only that relaxed boyish grin that was so like his
son's, which said he had shrugged off the other world
he moved in and sunk himself into the sheer relief from
it all that his family offered him.

But now she wondered if that same process worked
in reverse. She had never so much as considered it before
but, when Daniel walked out of the house, did he shrug
off the mantel of husband and father as easily? Was it
a relief to get back into that other, more exciting world
he moved in? Be the big man who wielded power over
others and was treated as someone very special? And
did the little woman and three small children at home
fade into nothing once he was back in the sophisticated
arena of sophisticated people with sophisticated intel-
lects, who wore sophisticated clothes and could converse
with him on his own sophisticated level?

Sophisticated, she repeated to herself for the ump-
teenth time. That was what Daniel had become—a ma-
tured and sophisticated man, while she had stagnated.

She hated herself for letting it happen. And she hated
Daniel for forcing her to see her own faults, because that
meant she had to shoulder some of the blame for what
was happening to them.

Rachel was inexplicably relieved that Daniel's black
BMW was not on the drive when her taxi dropped her
off at the house well after six o'clock that evening.

She struggled up the drive with her arms so loaded
with carrier bags and parcels that she had to ring the
doorbell with her elbow.

'Good heavens!' Daniel's mother exclaimed when she
opened the door, a look of complete disbelief on her

face as Rachel staggered inside the house. 'And—good heavens again!' she repeated when she lifted stunned eyes from the tumble of packages Rachel dropped at their feet and looked—really looked—at Rachel instead.

'What do you think?' Rachel quizzed uncertainly.

The Rachel who had left the house only an hour after her husband that morning was not the one now waiting anxiously for her mother-in-law's opinion.

Gone was the long mass of pale blond hair. It had been cut, ruthlessly cut, and styled to fall in a fine silken bob on a level with her small chin. Her face had been expertly made-up to enhance those good features Rachel did not believe she had. Everything had been kept so cleverly natural that it was almost impossible to tell what the difference was about her eyes and mouth, only that suddenly they leapt out and hit you in a way Jenny found wholly disturbing.

But that wasn't all. Gone was the baby-blue woollen duffle coat and faded jeans Rachel had gone out in, and in their place was the most exquisitely tailored pure wool coat-dress in a soft and sensual mink colour which followed her slender figure from lightly padded shoulders to the delicate curve of her calf. It fastened on two rows of large brown saucer-type buttons down its revered front, and again in a single row of three along the deep cuffs at her wrists. Her new three-inch-high brown suede ankle boots and purse matched the buttons.

'I think,' Jenny Masterson murmured, eventually, 'that we had better have a stiff drink ready for my son when he gets home.'

Jenny couldn't know it, but she had given the most satisfying reply Rachel could have wished for. But that was because she was still running on full pistons of defiance, and the longer she had been out today the stronger that defiance had become.

The sitting-room door came flying open and Sammy's gasped 'Wow!' made Rachel grin like an idiot. But if she had worried a little bit about how the children were going to react to this new mother they'd got, then it was a worry wasted.

'What's in the parcels?' he demanded, dismissing the new Rachel as if she was no different from the one he was used to seeing. And within ten minutes the sitting-room floor was littered with half-open packages, and Kate was strutting around in a set of red beads that Rachel had bought on impulse—along with the set of building bricks for Michael, who was now engrossed in tearing up the cardboard box they came in, and a new computer game for Sam, who had already shot off upstairs to try it out—when Daniel walked in.

He stopped and stared. And, with that, the room seemed to come to a shuddering halt as Kate stopped strutting to view his reaction, and his mother stopped trying to tidy up some of the mess to eye him warily while Rachel, caught in the middle of coming to her feet, had to force her suddenly shaky limbs to finish the move, then stood staring at Daniel in a mixture of mutinous defiance and helpless appeal.

It was his mother who broke the spell, bustling forward to scoop Michael up from the carpet, then grab Kate's hand to hustle them all from the room.

'Children see and feel more than grown-ups give them credit for,' Jenny had told Rachel only a few days earlier. No more, just that candid one-liner, but it had been enough. Rachel received the message. The children had obviously been saying things to their grandmother they felt they could not say to their parents.

But at this moment Rachel was not thinking of her children; her attention was turned entirely on Daniel's perfectly inscrutable expression as he ran his narrowed gaze over her.

As she watched him in growing tension she saw a small smile twist his lips. It jolted her because she recognised it as the same smile he had used on entering the disco all those years ago when they first met—one she read as rueful and cynical—and it had the effect of pushing up her chin and adding a touch of challenge to her expression.

'Well, well,' he murmured eventually. 'Stage two has begun, I see.'

Stage two? Rachel frowned. What was he talking about?

'Going somewhere nice?' he asked before she could question him. 'You'll have to forgive me, Rachel, but if you did warn me that you'd made plans to go out tonight, they seem to have completely slipped my mind.'

Her frown deepened, and the way he clipped out the 'nice' was enough to make her bristle. He was a man who never let anything slip his mind! It was like a bank vault; nothing that went into it got out again without his say-so! He knew damned well she was not going anywhere, so what was he getting at with his cryptic 'stage twos', and 'going somewhere nice'?

And it was obvious he wasn't going to make a single remark about her new look—the rotter! Perhaps he didn't like it—perhaps he preferred the boringly plain other version who wasn't likely to cause him much trouble, the one who knew her place in his well-ordered life and never thought of stepping beyond it!

Or perhaps he wasn't so sure of this Rachel! she then mused on a growing sense of triumph. Perhaps the enquiry was really genuine and he was wondering if she was going out somewhere!

'And if I am considering going out, what would you do about it?' she demanded.

That smile tilted his mouth again and sent a trickle of angry frustration shooting down her spine. 'I would have to ask you who you are going with, I suppose,' he drawled, better at this game than she could ever be.

'So you could vet him—or her—to see if they're suitable company for your little wife?'

'Him?' He grabbed at that and threw it back sharply, sharply enough to make her sting in satisfaction. 'And just who is—he?' he demanded softly.

'I don't remember your having to inform me of every person you've ever gone out with,' she countered coolly.

His face tightened, grey eyes flashing a brief warning at her before he hooded them again. 'Humour me,' he requested. 'Give me a name—that's all—a name.'

This was a stupid conversation since she was going absolutely nowhere! she realised suddenly, and sighed, her shoulders slumping inside the soft mink wool. 'There isn't a name,' she muttered, angry at the easy way he had managed totally to deflate her exciting day. Her eyes glittered around the scattered parcels which had now lost all their pleasure. 'I'm on my way in, not out.' And one look at this room made it as clear as night followed day that she had just come in from a long day's shopping spree! Who was he trying to kid with that small frown that suggested he was only just noticing the mad clutter of boxes, bags and tissue-paper?

Daniel moved across the room to the nearest one—a long, flat box which had not yet been delved into by curious fingers—and Rachel took her chance while he was no longer blocking her exit, picked up her new brown suede bag and moved towards the sitting-room door, her mouth set in a thin line of disappointment.

'What's in this?'

She shrugged, feeling as petulant as Kate did when she did not get the response she had been anticipating. 'A suit,' she answered reluctantly.

'And this one?' He nudged another box with a highly polished shoe.

'Underwear.' She blushed uncomfortably, because the box was full to overflowing with the most expensive silk underwear Rachel had ever seen.

'And this?'

'A couple of new dresses!' Her eyes flashed resentfully at him. 'Why?' she demanded. 'You aren't going to read me a lecture on over-spending are you? It was you who gave me all those credit card things! One for every big store in London, I think!' She had a wallet stuffed with them. They had just taken up space in her purse until today, when she had learned the delights they could offer her.

He ignored that, his expression slightly guarded when he suggested casually enough, 'A dress worthy of dinner in one of London's most exclusive restaurants, with maybe a little dancing later?'

She had turned back to the door by this time, but the invitation had her spinning back to stare at him in blank incomprehension. 'Are you asking me out?' she queried, with such a blatant lack of guile that Daniel's smile became ruefully crooked.

'Yes.' He nodded, all dry mockery. And Rachel had a feeling that he found her lack of sophistication highly amusing. She flushed heatedly, wishing the world would just open up and swallow her rather than continue to put her through this purgatory. Nothing she could do, it seemed, would ever make her anything more than a silly, gauche fool! 'Yes, Rachel,' he repeated more gently, as though reading her discomfort and suddenly sorry for causing it. 'I am asking you if you would like to dine out with me tonight.'

'Oh.' Thoroughly disconcerted, and not sure how to answer him, she was very relieved when Sam came tumbling down the stairs at that moment, like a snowball out of control, to rumble right by her and leap like a jack-rabbit on to his father's chest.

'Hi!' he greeted, smiling into that face which was so like his own. 'Mum's got me this great new computer game,' he went on in an excited rush. 'Can I bring it down here and try it out on the big TV? It's a flight simulator and you have to take off and land a Tornado jet!'

'Why not?' Daniel agreed, smiling at his son while his eyes never left Rachel. 'If your grandmother doesn't mind, that is, since she will be staying here with you while I take your mother out to dinner.'

'You're taking Mum out?' The child sounded as surprised as Rachel had been, which made Daniel grimace. But Sam was already beaming his approval at Rachel. 'That's great!' he announced. 'Dad taking you out instead of you going on your own like last——'

'Sam.' The quiet warning from his father shut him up, and Rachel felt stiff and awkward.

'Maybe your mother doesn't want to baby-sit,' she said uncomfortably, knowing he had only asked her because he felt obliged to after seeing all the trouble she'd gone to to make herself different. 'She's been here all day as it is. It isn't fair to——'

'I don't mind,' another voice chipped in quietly from the hallway. Rachel turned to find his mother and Kate standing there, listening in as if there was no such thing as privacy in this house!

'That's not the point!' Rachel snapped. 'You've been put on quite enough for one day. I——'

'Take her somewhere nice,' Jenny said to her son over the top of Rachel's protests.

Rachel sighed impatiently because she was well aware that she was being thoroughly outmanoeuvred here. 'I haven't said I want to go out, as far as I recall!' she inserted crossly.

'Of course you want to go!' Jenny dismissed that argument. 'So just get upstairs with you—and take all those boxes with you!' she ordered. 'Kate—Sammy—help your mother upstairs with some of these,' she continued briskly, while Rachel heaved a small sigh of surrender because, unless she was prepared to tell all of them why she had no wish to go anywhere with Daniel, she really had no choice.

The children jumped eagerly to their grandmother's bidding, gathering up parcels and making for the door, leaving Rachel to bring the rest. She was just starting up the stairs when Jenny's voice drifted towards her, sounding cross and stern. 'If you ask me, Daniel, this evening out for both of you is well overdue! And it wouldn't go amiss if you began involving her in your business socialising too!'

Pausing on the stairs, Rachel waited curiously to hear Daniel's reply to that stern scold, but his voice was pitched too low for her to catch the words.

But Jenny could be heard plainly. 'Rubbish!' she snapped. 'How do you know she'll hate it when you've never given her the chance to find out for herself? The trouble with you, Daniel, is you've kept her so wrapped up in cotton wool that she's never been allowed to discover what she wants out of life!'

Was that what Jenny really thought? Rachel mused curiously. She'd always thought she knew exactly what she wanted out of life—to be a wife and mother. That was all. Nothing fancy. Nothing ambitious or over-exciting. Just a wife to the man she loved and a mother to the children she adored.

Was there something wrong with that?

'And I'll have my say about something else, while I'm about it,' Jenny continued brusquely. 'I don't know what has been happening here to break that poor child's heart, but I know her blessed eyes have been opened to something nasty—and I know where the blame for that lies too!'

Rachel felt her heart sink, that horrible feeling of desolation washing over her as it always did when she was reminded of Mandy's call.

Lights really do go out when your world caves in, she observed sadly.

'Take my advice, son,' Jenny was saying, 'and tread very carefully from now on. Because if Rachel ever...'

Rachel ran. She didn't want to know what would happen if Rachel ever! What was happening right now to Rachel was more than enough to contend with with-out worrying about what would happen if Rachel ever...!

# CHAPTER SIX

IF RACHEL ever—what? she found herself wondering later, while she hovered in Michael's small bathroom waiting for Daniel to finish in their bedroom so that she could sneak in there and get ready without having to come face to face with him again.

If Rachel ever found out about his other women? Well, Rachel had already done that.

If Rachel ever decided to grow up? she then pondered cynically, catching a glimpse of her new self in the bathroom mirror and almost doing a double-take because it was like looking at a total stranger!

And just look at you! she told that reflection. Hiding away in here when you don't even need to use the bathroom! You daren't bath in case the steam ruins your new hairstyle. You daren't wash because you aren't confident enough to re-do your clever make-up. Daniel is taking you out—but only because of some reason of his own which has to hinge on his guilty conscience! And he's expecting to take out that other person he met downstairs—the same one you're staring at right now—when really she's just an illusion! A disguise the real Rachel is trying to hide behind!

She heard a door open and close, then Daniel's distinctive tread as he made his way back down the stairs. With a deep breath and a harried glance at the woman in the mirror, she let herself out of her hiding place. Over her arm lay one of the new dresses she had bought that day, and she hung it on the wardrobe door, then stood back to harry herself over whether she dared wear it or not.

It was a rather disturbingly sexy thing, made of a dark ruby lace lined in fine black silk. It had a heart-shaped bodice held up by two rather flimsy-looking bootlace straps, and the delicate fabric clung almost lovingly in sensual lacy scollops across the creamy slope of her breasts. It left her arms and shoulders bare—and the best part of her back, she recalled, giving the dress a twitch with her hand to remind herself just how low it dipped at the back. The assistant had seen her uncertain expression when Rachel had realised just how much of her skin it revealed, and had rushed off to come back with a black velvet bolero with long fitted sleeves, a small stand-up collar and two curving front panels, which left the seductive dip of ruby lace between her breasts tantalisingly exposed.

So, did she wear it? she wondered pensively. Or did she revert to the black dress hanging in the wardrobe that she usually wore when she went out with Daniel?

Kate slipped into the bedroom, looking all rosy pink and smelling of talcum powder. She came to stand beside Rachel, her blue eyes widening on the new dress.

'Is that what you're going to wear?' she asked in soft awe.

'I don't know,' Rachel answered uncertainly. 'Maybe—maybe I should just fall back on my black dress...' Her hand went to draw the other dress from the wardrobe when Kate stopped her.

'But you can't wear that!' she exclaimed, sounding horrified. 'Daddy is all dressed up in his penguin suit and bow tie! He looks fantastic!'

Rachel's lips twitched; obviously Kate's fantastic daddy deserved something better than the black dress.

'That old black thing is boring, anyway,' her daughter added.

Boring, Rachel repeated to herself. Now there's a word she had become very familiar with over the last few weeks. 'Then the red it is,' she drily agreed. The old Rachel was boring; this new one was determined not to be! 'Now you go and help Grandma with Michael while I get myself ready.' She dropped a kiss on her daughter's cheek then watched her scamper off—eager, it seemed to Rachel, to be as much help as she could to see her parents go out and enjoy themselves.

Well...she thought a trifle breathlessly as she paused outside the sitting-room door. She had been suitably drooled over by all those in the kitchen playing snap. All she had to do now was steady her stuttering heart and go and face the real expert!

Kate was right, she observed as she slipped quietly into the room, Daniel did look fantastic in his black dinner-jacket. But it was more than just the superb cut of the cloth. It was the man inside it that made all the difference. There was an air of maturity and sophistication about him which only seemed to increase that innate sex-appeal he had always possessed. He was over by the drinks tray, his face turned away from her as he poured himself a simple tonic water. He hadn't realised she'd come into the room yet, and Rachel was glad because it gave her a few moments to steady the effect he had on her senses. His thick dark hair was as neat and semi-casual as it always was, neither too short nor too long, fashionable or old-fashioned. But then, that spoke a lot about his character. Daniel had always stamped his impact on people with a clever balance between the conventional and the unconventional. A man of super-confidence—underplayed. And intimidating for it, because there was so much of the real person he liked to keep hidden.

He was intimidating her now as she stood there nervously fingering the lip of her black velvet bolero. He had never used to make her feel like this—in fact, she had never used to think of Daniel as anything but the man she loved. And it was yet another first she had to contend with, that she could actually feel overawed by a man she had lived and slept with for seven years of her life.

He was a stranger to her, she realised with a painful start. A stranger living beneath an umbrella of close intimacy. Had it always been like that? she wondered. Then she went cold inside as the answer came back to her, clear and cruel in its honesty. Yes, it had always been like that. Daniel was the stranger she had loved blindly, married blindly, and lived with blindly for seven whole years.

Was he aware that she didn't know him, really know him, for the man he was out there beyond these cloistered walls? And if he did know, did it matter to him much? Or had he been quite content to live the dual life of family man and dynamic tycoon where one role did not intrude on the other?

He turned then and saw her standing there, and her heart gave another painful twist as she watched him narrow his eyes so that she could not read their expression as he ran them slowly over her.

He hides away from me, she realised. He does it all the time. Even now, as he ran his gaze from the top of her gleaming new hairstyle and her perfectly made-up face which did so much to enhance all those beautiful features even Rachel herself was not aware she possessed, he revealed nothing of himself. The dress was different, far more sophisticated than anything she had ever worn before. It accentuated her slender figure, the long graceful line of her legs. Daniel took it all in without showing a single hint of what he was thinking behind his urbane mask.

Then, without any warning, his lashes flickered, and there was a flash of emotion before he had severely dismissed it again.

Hurt. It startled her because she was sure she saw hurt in that expression then! But why should he be hurting because his wife was standing here dressed up to go out with him?

Or maybe it wasn't hurt, but guilty conscience which caused that spasm. What was it his mother had said? 'You've kept her so wrapped up in cotton wool.' And that must have hit him on the raw, just as looking at her standing here like this, different, yet still the same Rachel inside, was hitting his conscience, because he must know she would never have gone to these extremes to make herself different if he had not made her feel so damned uncertain of the person she had always believed herself to be!

'Drink before we go?' he asked.

He wasn't going to comment. She felt like a balloon slowly deflating from a central prick with a pin. 'No—thank you,' she refused, damning her voice for sounding husky. 'Did...did you manage to reserve a table somewhere?'

His twisted smile seemed to mock her for some reason. 'I managed,' he said. 'Shall we go then?'

Oh, let's not bother! Rachel thought with silent resentment as she turned to walk out of the sitting-room door.

She sat stiffly beside him, watching his long fingers control the car as the BMW accelerated towards London. She rarely rode in this car because when they went out together it was usually as a family, and since it was her white Escort which had been fitted out with all the correct safety gear to take the children, that was the one they usually used. So she felt strange riding in the BMW—

strange with everything, she acknowledged heavily, even herself.

'Where are we going?' she asked with little enthusiasm.

She felt his glance brush her and looked round at him in time to see his jaw tighten as he turned back to the road. He named a club-cum-restaurant that made her skin prickle with alarm. It was one of those well-known places which the rich and famous generally frequented. She'd always believed you needed a celebrity status to get into places like it. The fact that Daniel was tossing off the name as though it were nothing increased her mood of discomfort.

'The food's good,' he was saying casually. 'Good enough to tempt even the frailest appetites...'

Was that meant for her? It could have been, she conceded. She was well aware that her appetite had been sadly missing recently. But then food was a problem to swallow when you lived with a permanent lump in your throat.

'You've been there before, then,' she surmised.

'Once or twice.'

With Lydia? She could not stop the thought from coming and, once there, it left her quiet and even more subdued for the rest of the journey.

If Daniel noticed he didn't bother remarking on it, his own mood not much better than her own as he guided her into the foyer, where clever lighting enhanced the luxury of their surroundings.

'Good evening, Mr Masterson.' A short rotund man with a bald head and dark French eyes appeared like magic in front of them. He bowed politely to Rachel, who smiled jerkily in return.

'Good evening, Claude,' Daniel was saying in a familiar way which made Rachel grimace. 'Good of you to fit us in at such short notice.'

Claude gave a typically European shrug. 'You know how it is sir. Some people you always have room for. This way, please...'

Daniel's hand came to her waist, his fingers settling in an intimate curve of her ribcage as he propelled her forwards. Trying not to look awed by the elegance of her surroundings, she looked around her as Claude took them through to a restaurant that was nothing like any restaurant she had ever been in before.

On the other occasions when Daniel had taken her out it had usually been to one of the local places, Indian or Chinese or Italian, where he could wear a pair of his casual trousers and a polo shirt under his sports jacket, and she could wear something equally casual. They would lounge in their seats and share a meal and a bottle of wine with the relaxed intimacy of two people who felt comfortable in each other's company. But here Rachel could not imagine daring to lounge in her seat. Just as she couldn't imagine Daniel pinching a prawn off her plate if the mood took him, or herself leaning across the table to feed one to him, because she knew his insatiable love of prawns meant he would suck it greedily from her fingers.

The mood here did not encourage that kind of relaxed intimacy. In fact, she realised as the awe wore off to be replaced with something closely resembling contempt, she thought the place rather lacked atmosphere of any kind but the We-eat-here-because-it-is-fashionable-to-eat-here kind.

'You don't like it.' She glanced up to find Daniel watching her expression.

'It all looks very—nice,' she replied.

'Nice,' Daniel huffed out sardonically. 'This happens to be one of the finest restaurants in London, and you call it—nice.'

'I'm sorry.' She looked at him. 'Am I supposed to be suitably impressed?'

'No.' That nerve twitched in his jaw.

'Or maybe I'm supposed to be impressed with your ability to get in here at short notice?' she suggested. 'Be careful, Daniel,' she drawled, 'or I might even begin to suspect that you're trying to impress me.'

'And that is just too ridiculous to contemplate, is it?'

She thought about that, her gaze drifting among the other tables where people sat in their elegant clothes with their elegant faces wearing elegant expressions. Then she looked back at Daniel.

'Frankly, yes,' she replied, her mouth taking on a self-derisive slant. 'I thought we both knew that you've never had to do anything to impress me.'

He sighed impatiently. 'Rachel. I didn't bring you here to argue with you. I only wanted to——'

'Give me a special treat?' she suggested sardonically.

'No!' he denied. 'I wanted to please you—please you!' he repeated with a bitter-soft ferocity.

'By showing how your other half lives?' she mocked.

'My other half?' He looked genuinely nonplussed. 'What the hell is that supposed to mean?'

'The other you I know nothing about,' she shrugged, adding heavily to herself, The Daniel who's grown stronger while the other one has been slowly fading away before my very eyes without my noticing it. 'The one who feels perfectly at ease in places like this.'

His grey eyes flashed her an impatient look. 'Would you rather we had gone to the local Chinese dressed like this?' he derided. 'You went to a lot of trouble today to create your new image, Rachel. This——' his gaze flicked briefly around their surroundings '—suits the new image. It's up to you to decide whether you prefer it or not.'

Not, she thought, then grimaced when her heart gave a dull thump in acknowledgement of what that answer meant. This was not her, dressed for the part or not. But it was so obviously Daniel that she wanted to weep. Had they anything in common left worth hanging on to?

'And do you prefer it?' she asked him curiously. 'The new image?' she enlightened his puzzled frown.

He sat back in his seat, his eyes wearing an odd expression as they ran over her. 'I like the new hairstyle,' he admitted after a moment, 'but I'm not sure I like your reasons for doing it. I like the dress,' he went on, before she could respond. 'It's beautiful—as you probably well know—but I don't like what it does to the woman I——'

A waiter appeared at her side, effectively cutting Daniel off mid-word as he placed a glass of something cool and clear in front of Rachel then offered the same to Daniel. 'Your menus, sir,' he murmured, opening the dark green leather-backed menus and presenting them with one each.

'Thank you,' Daniel said, abruptly dismissing the man with a curt flick of a finger. The waiter bowed politely, then left them.

'You were very short with him,' Rachel censured. 'What did he do to make you behave so rudely?'

'He interrupted me while I was trying to compliment you.'

She sent him a deriding look. 'If you call those compliments, Daniel, then I'm certainly not impressed with your style!'

He grimaced ruefully. 'All right,' he conceded, 'so I'm finding it difficult to come to terms with the new you. Rachel——' he leaned forward suddenly, his gaze urgent as he took hold of one of her hands '—you're beautiful, you don't need me to tell you that——'

Don't I? she questioned wryly.

'But don't—please don't lose the lovely person you were before in your effort to prove something to me!'

'I didn't do this for you, Daniel,' she informed him coldly. 'I did it for myself. It was time, after all,' she added bleakly, 'that I grew up.'

'Oh, no, darling,' he murmured thickly, 'you're so wrong! I——'

'Well, Daniel Masterson, as I live and breathe!' a smoothly sardonic voice drawled.

'Damn!' Daniel muttered, his grip tightening on Rachel's hand before he let go of her abruptly, schooled his expression into a fascinatingly bland mask, then looked up into the face of their intruder.

'Zac,' he acknowledged, coming smoothly to his feet. 'I thought you were in the States.'

He stepped from behind their table to shake the other man's hand, and Rachel glanced up to find herself gazing into the attractive face of a man around Daniel's age. He was rake-thin and blond, with a pair of bright green eyes that appeared sharp enough to cut armour-plating if he wanted them to.

'Been back several weeks now,' he replied. 'It's you who seem to have been out of circulation recently...' His glance swept curiously down towards Rachel—then darkened with pure male interest. 'Could this beautiful creature be the reason why?' he mused softly. Then, boldly to Daniel, 'So what happened to the lovely L——?'

'My wife,' Daniel cut in, editing out whatever the other man had been going to say—but not before Rachel had added the last word for herself. 'Rachel.' With what seemed to her a very reluctant move, he shifted to one side to place her in full view of the newcomer. 'This is Zac Callum. We use the same legal firm,' he concluded tautly.

Zac Callum threw Daniel a sharply speculative look. 'Don't we just?' Rachel thought she heard him murmur beneath his breath as he stepped by Daniel's stiff frame to hold out his hand to her.

But she was too busy repeating his name to herself to find time to wonder what that soft remark could mean, because the name she knew. He was the political cartoonist for the *Sunday Globe*, and cruelly witty he was too. He had an unerring ability to latch on to people's weak points and use them to turn even the most prominent person into a laughing stock, which also made him quite a TV celebrity. He tended to turn up on quiz shows and the like, adding a bit of wicked spice to the proceedings.

'No wonder Daniel has been noticeable for his absence over the last few weeks,' he murmured as Rachel placed her hand in his. Long, incredibly slender fingers closed over hers. 'A wife,' he added softly. 'Your taste has certainly improved, Daniel.'

He means Lydia, Rachel thought wretchedly. 'Thank you,' she said, answering for Daniel. He looked so tense that she had a suspicion he wouldn't be able to speak even if he wanted to. 'I—I've heard of you, Mr Callum,' she told him shyly. 'I enjoy your work.'

'A fan?' His eyes began to glint with humour. 'Tell me more...' Gripping the back of a vacant chair, he went to pull it out from beneath the table.

'Zac, darling—aren't you forgetting something?' a wry voice intruded.

Pulling a rueful face exclusively for Rachel's benefit, he straightened, then turned towards the woman standing just behind him. 'Sorry,' he apologised. 'But you must understand, this is a moment to be savoured. This man, of all men, surrendering to the wedded trap.' His sigh was explicit, as was the taunting expression he turned on Daniel. 'Claire.' Placing a hand around his companion's slender waist, he drew her forward. 'This is Daniel Masterson of whom you no doubt have already heard.'

'Who hasn't?' she said drily. 'We all waited with bated breath for the outcome of the Harvey bid.'

The Harvey bid. Rachel lowered her eyes, wondering if she was the only person in the world who didn't know just how important the Harvey thing had been.

'Nice to meet you,' Claire was saying, while Daniel only acknowledged her with a slight impression of a smile. His hard gaze was fixed on Zac Callum, who was still eyeing Rachel with undiluted interest.

'We would ask you to join us, but we've already ordered,' Daniel lied. 'And...' He left the rest unsaid, but it was obvious to all of them Daniel did not want them intruding.

'Don't worry.' Zac laughed—a pleasant, huskily teasing sound. 'We have no wish to gate-crash on newly-weds.'

At last Daniel opened his mouth to contest the mistake—then caught Rachel's gaze and was silenced.

Don't, her eyes pleaded with him. Don't tell them the truth! He knows about Lydia. Don't put me up for ridicule by telling them you've had a wife for seven years and children for six when he obviously knows about your mistress!

Grimly he looked down and away, his mouth thinning even more in angry frustration with the whole unwanted scene.

Which only made her feel worse, so out of her depth here that she wanted to run away and hide—hide in choking humiliation.

Then Daniel did a strange thing. He reached out for her, capturing her chin with a hand as he suddenly bent his own dark head towards her. And there, among London's best and most sophisticated, he kissed her, hot and possessively. And when he released her surprised mouth his eyes were so darkened by pain that it brought tears springing into Rachel's own.

'The honeymoon is obviously not over,' mocked Zac Callum. 'Come on, Claire. I think we should leave these two love-birds alone.'

'What do you want to eat?'

Miles away, feeling hot and flustered by Daniel's unexpected kiss, and unbearably moved by that revealing expression in his eyes, Rachel had to force herself to concentrate on what he had said. He was back in his seat, guarded eyes watching her intently.

'I...' She looked down at the menu in front of her, the list of dishes blurring into illegibility. 'I...' Her heart was stammering in her breast, the nervous tip of her pink tongue desperate to flick around lips still burning from his kiss. 'You order for me,' she invited in the end, tossing the menu aside because it was no use her trying to make sense of it feeling as she did.

Grimly he made a small gesture that brought the waiter scuttling over, then ordered in a curt clipped voice that had the waiter nodding nervously before scuttling away again as if the tension at the table was too much to stand near for long.

Had the waiter seen Daniel kiss her? Had the whole room? Cheeks heating, Rachel cast a furtive glance around her to find everyone seemingly engrossed in their own interests rather than theirs. Knotting her hands together beneath the cover of the oyster-pink tablecloth, she made herself speak normally.

'How do you know Zac Callum?' she asked.

He gave an indifferent shrug. 'He inherited a couple of small companies from his father,' he explained. 'He didn't want them, so he sold them to me.'

'I like his work,' she remarked. 'It was a medium I was rather good at myself, so I find I can appreciate the gift he has.'

'Appreciate his charm, too, did you?' Daniel clipped out tightly.

Rachel's eyes widened, surprised by the unveiled green-eyed jealousy she heard in his tone.

Daniel—jealous of another man looking at her? The mind boggled on the concept. 'Is that why you kissed me like that?' she demanded.

A sudden blindingly bitter look shot across his gaze. 'He was eyeing you up like a tasty new dish on the damned menu,' he gritted. 'I wanted there to be no mistake about who you belonged to.'

Belonged? She belonged to Daniel, but Daniel apparently did not belong to her, if Lydia was a gauge in belonging. 'Does anyone in this other world you move in know about me and the children?' she asked heavily then.

He took exception to her reference to his other world, but bit the bullet on it. 'My private life is none of their business,' he said brusquely. 'I mix with them purely for business' sake, that's all. Now can we drop the subject?' he snapped. 'Unless of course you found Zac Callum's charm more appealing than my company, in which case I'll call him back if you like, and you can both flatter each other's egos a little bit more!'

Oh, he was jealous! The idea certainly gave her flagging ego an enormous boost. 'Well, at least he didn't snap his dining companion's head off every time she opened her mouth,' she taunted sweetly, watching with a growing sense of pleased triumph as dark colour slid across his cheeks at the rebuke.

Their first course arrived then, thankfully, because sitting here in public with him like this, when really all they both seemed to want to do was snap out taunts at each other, made eating the better option.

He'd ordered her a light salmon mousse that made her mouth water when she had believed she wouldn't be able to eat a single morsel of food. And she was halfway through when Daniel reached across the table and touched her gently on the back of her hand.

'Rachel,' he murmured huskily, bringing her wary gaze up to clash with his. 'Can we at least try to make this a pleasant evening for us both?' he pleaded. 'I don't want to fight with you. I want——'

'Daniel—how nice to see you!'

His face darkened with irritation, and Rachel herself felt a stab of disappointment at the new interruption because she had been allowing herself the rare pleasure of drowning in the smoky urgency of his beautiful eyes.

This time he didn't get up to greet the middle-aged couple who had stopped by their table. Nor did he introduce her. He just made all the right polite noises, but in a way that had them quickly moving on.

'Now you know why I don't like bringing you to places like this,' he grimaced. 'We are destined to be interrupted like this all evening.'

'And what's wrong with that?' she asked, bristling because she saw his impatience as reluctance to acknowledge her here for what she was to him.

'Because when I take you out, I like to have you to myself!' he said, and that look was back in his eyes, that darkly smouldering, intensely possessive one that turned her stomach inside out and made eating anything else a near-impossibility.

But he was right. They were interrupted no less than three more times during the course of their meal, and in the end Daniel sighed and reached across the table for her hand to draw her with him as he stood up.

'Come on,' he said. 'We may as well go through to the club and dance. At least while we're dancing people will be reluctant to interrupt.'

Keeping hold of her hand, he threaded his way through the tables towards a pair of closed doors that swung open at the touch of his free hand. It was darker in here; from the entrance she could just see through the gloom to the opposite side of the room, which had its own bar and a small raised stage where a group of musicians sat playing slow, easy jazz.

Daniel drew her on to the dance-floor and turned her into his arms. Instantly she was assailed by a weird feeling of nervous uncertainty—as if he were a stranger, the kind of tall, dark stranger that appealed to her senses and made her excruciatingly aware of herself as a woman.

This is Daniel, she reminded herself fiercely as he began to sway with her to the music. No stranger, but the man you've been married to for seven years.

But this Daniel was a stranger to her, she acknowledged heavily. And not only because she was here with him in his other world, so to speak. They had become strangers weeks ago—estranged while still living together as man and wife.

A sigh broke from her. The sadness in it must have reached Daniel, because the hand covering hers where it lay against the smooth lapel of his dinner-jacket squeezed, and his other moved on her waist, sliding up and beneath her black bolero with the intention of pressing her closer—then stopped, a sudden breathless stillness assailing both of them as his fingers made surprised contact with warm bare flesh.

She'd forgotten the backless design of the dress until that moment, had been uptight about too many other things to care about something she'd had no intention of revealing. But she remembered now and had to close her eyes as a wild wave of sensation rippled right through her.

She tried to fight it, moving her head in an effort to take in air that was not filled with the musky sensual smell of him emanating up from his warm throat. But he stopped her, the hand holding hers lifting to curve her nape, pressing her back against him.

'*Déjà vu*,' Daniel whispered, and she gasped out an unsteady breath when she realised what he meant.

The first time they'd ever danced together she'd been wearing a little cropped T-shirt that he'd slipped his fingers beneath. This time it was a velvet bolero, more elegant, more sophisticated, but her reaction was the same.

Hot and drenching, a sexual awareness that sizzled like liquid on burning coals. Her heart hammered in response, and as she stiffened on a fizz of sensation his fingertips began to graze lightly along her spine.

No, she told herself breathlessly. Don't let him do this to you!

But the fine hairs covering her body began to tingle in pleasurable response to his caress, forcing her eyes to close and her spine to move into a supple arch that sent the sensitive tips of her breasts brushing against the heated wall of his chest. She felt Daniel's body tighten against her, harden, begin to throb with a need older than time itself, and let out a shakily helpless sigh.

His dark head lowered to nuzzle her throat. 'It hasn't changed one iota, has it?' he breathed. 'We still have this amazing effect on each other.'

He was, oh, so right. And on a final sigh that came from deep, deep inside her, she surrendered to it all, letting herself do what she was desperate to do, and stretched up to brush her mouth softly against his.

It was the first time in long weeks that she had made a voluntary move towards him, and he acknowledged it with a rasping intake of air, his lean body shuddering as he released the air again.

'Let's go home,' he said hoarsely. 'This isn't what I want to be doing with you.'

'I...' All right, she was about to concede, feeling as if she had nothing left to fight him with. But then another acidly mocking, shudderingly familiar voice intruded, and everything within her seemed to shatter into a thousand broken pieces.

'Well, if it isn't Don Juan himself. And with a brand-new conquest too...'

# CHAPTER SEVEN

RACHEL closed her eyes, a dark wave of recognition making her blonde head drop wearily on to Daniel's shoulder while he stiffened like a board.

'You do know he's married, don't you, dear?' the cruel voice taunted.

Obviously Mandy had not recognised the new Rachel in the woman Daniel was holding in his arms.

'For seven long years, no less,' she went on regardless. 'To a pretty, if insipid, little thing, who will be sitting at home at this very moment, taking care of their three sweet children while her darling husband plays lover to any woman who will have him.'

'Oh, not just anyone, Amanda,' Daniel countered coldly. 'I always found it very easy to turn you down, after all.'

Mandy wanted Daniel? Lifting her face, Rachel stared into his harshly cynical eyes and felt something else rend apart inside her as yet another veil was ripped from her blind, trusting eyes. Daniel watched it happen with a grim clenching of his jaw.

Daniel and Mandy did not get on; she had always accepted that as one of those things, without bothering to question why they were so hostile towards each other. Well, now she knew, and she felt sick with the knowledge.

'Man must always beware of a woman scorned, Daniel,' Mandy cautioned sagely. 'It is one of our most—destructive little weapons, after all.'

'And you used it so well, didn't you?' Daniel drawled. 'Aiming directly at the weakest point.'

'How is Rachel, by the way?' she drawled. 'Has the poor thing any idea how quickly you've found a replacement for the ousted Lydia?'

Enough. Rachel had heard enough. Twisting within the constricting grasp of Daniel's arms, she turned to look at her once-best friend, watching with a complete lack of expression as all the colour left Mandy's face; without saying a word, Mandy spun gracefully on her heel and walked away.

The mood was shot, the evening a disaster. Neither spoke as they left the club and walked the short distance to where Daniel had parked the car.

Then, 'How long?' she asked, once he'd slid the car into the steady stream of traffic leaving London.

'Years,' he shrugged, not even trying to misunderstand her.

'Did you ever take her up on it?'

As she watched him she saw his fingers take a white-knuckled grip on the steering wheel, his mouth tightening because the question offended his dignity, but he had to accept her right to ask it. 'No,' he answered flatly. 'Never even considered it.'

'Why not?'

'She leaves me cold,' he replied dismissively.

And it was a dismissal, one Rachel had to believe simply by the sheer lack of feeling with which he said it.

'Then why didn't you tell me what she was trying to do?'

'And ruin your faith in someone you cared a great deal for?' He sent her a sombre glance. 'I never hid the fact that I thoroughly disliked her, Rachel,' he reminded her grimly.

'But you never went out of your way to discourage the friendship either,' she pointed out. 'One word—one word, Daniel,' she emphasised tightly, 'that she was only using me to get to you, and tonight's little scene could have been avoided.'

'Knowing how deeply the truth would hurt you?' His expression was harsh in the dim light inside the car. 'I would have had to be some kind of heel to do that to you, Rachel.'

'True,' she conceded, and left that single word hanging in the air between them, knowing he had read the other meaning it offered—and knowing he had no defence against it.

She entered the house first, making directly for the stairs without bothering to go in and speak to Jenny. 'I have a headache,' she mumbled, which was not exactly a lie. There were a lot of different bits aching inside her, her head only one of them. 'Please apologise to your mother for me.'

She was not asleep when Daniel eventually came to bed after taking his mother home. But she pretended to be, while intensely aware of every move he made around the quiet room as he prepared for bed. He came into it naked as he always did, lying on his back with his head supported on his arms, staring at the darkened ceiling while she lay very still beside him, wishing with all her aching heart that fate would just wave a hand across them and dismiss the last few weeks as if they had not happened.

But of course fate was not that kind or that forgiving, and they lay there like that for ages, the tension so thick in the darkened room that Rachel began to feel suffocated by it. Then Daniel let out a sigh and reached for her. She went unresistingly into his arms, needing what he was going to offer with probably as much desperation as he did. And their loving took on a silent frenzy which was almost as unbearable as the tense silence had been.

Lydia came to visit her again that night, stiffening her passion-racked body just at the point where she'd begun to believe she was going to gain release form her pent-up desires at last. Daniel felt the change in her, and went very still while he watched her fight the devils which were haunting her.

And she did fight, eyes closed over wretched tears, kiss-softened mouth quivering, her fingers biting into his muscle-locked shoulders.

Another obstacle climbed, she thought, with no sense of triumph when, for once, she managed to thrust Lydia away. And, on a shaky sigh, she pulled Daniel's mouth down to hers.

'Rachel,' he whispered as he entered her. Just, 'Rachel,' over and over again in a raw shaken way which said he had understood the battle she had just fought and won, and knew too that she had done it for his sake. For him.

Yet though they climbed together, and although their bodies throbbed to a mutual drum-beat of growing fulfilment, when it came to it Daniel leaped alone, leaving her feeling lost and empty. A failure in so many ways she did not dare count them.

Daniel became very busy—another take-over deal—and he had to spend nights away from home in negotiation with a small engineering company near Huddersfield. Rachel accepted his word with a tight-lipped refusal to comment, which sent him off tense-faced with angry frustration while she sat at home and tormented herself with suspicions she knew were unfair even while she allowed them free rein in her wretched aching soul. That Daniel in turn refused to comment on what he knew she was thinking told her that he had decided not to justify his every move to her. He was, in short, demanding that she trust him. But she couldn't, which only helped to pile the strain on their marriage. And life became hardly bearable over the next few weeks.

Then one afternoon she happened to be glancing through the local paper that dropped through her letter-box once a week, and saw something there that set her pulses humming.

Zac Callum was giving a talk about his work at the local college of art that evening, and anyone who was interested was invited to go along.

Daniel was away. But if she got his mother in to baby-sit, then it wouldn't hurt anyone if she went along, would it?

But, deep down, she knew she was only going out of a rebellious need to hit Daniel on the raw.

His own fault, she defended her reasoning as she guided her white Escort into a vacant parking slot outside the centre. He shouldn't have let her see that he could be jealous of someone like Zac Callum. It was only knowing that which had given her the incentive to come at all!

Slipping into the small assembly hall where the talk was going to be held, she took a seat close to the back, not expecting Zac to notice her or, even if he did, to recognise her. They had met only briefly, after all.

Yet he did notice her—and recognised her instantly. He walked on to the raised podium, glanced smilingly around the three-quarters-full room, saw her, paused, focused on her again, then made her blush by widening his smile so that everyone present turned to see whom he was personally acknowledging.

Her answering smile was shy and self-conscious, and she sank herself deeper into her pale blue duffle coat with a wish to fade away completely.

But once he began talking she started to relax again, finding herself caught up in the clever, quick, witty way he explained how he homed in on the weaknesses of his victims. He was relaxed and generous with his smiles, easy to laugh with, a clever entertainer as well as a good speaker.

Several times he caught her laughing with everyone else and winked at her, his familiarity giving a boost to an ego that had been sadly flagging over the last few weeks.

Afterwards he came straight to her, lightly fielding any remarks made to him as he made his way down the aisle to where she was standing preparing to leave.

'Rachel——' his warm fingers made a light clasp around her own '—how nice of you to come.'

'I'm glad I did.' She smiled, feeling stupidly shy and self-conscious again. 'You made it all sound so interesting.'

'Do you attend classes at this college?'

Her eyes widened. 'No!' she denied, flushing a little because it had never occurred to her that he would make such an assumption. But then she realised how she must look tonight in faded jeans and a casual duffle coat, her face completely free of make-up.

Nothing like the woman he had met as the wife of the dynamic Daniel Masterson, anyway. And probably more like a student.

'We live not far from here,' she explained. 'I read about tonight in the local newspaper and decided to come along on impulse.'

'By yourself?'

'Yes.' The flush deepened, why, she wasn't sure, since this man could have no idea that this was an unusual diversion for the stay-at-home Rachel to make. 'Daniel is away on business.'

'Ah.' As if that seemed to say it all, he sent her a strange look. 'Interested in politics?'

She shook her pale head. 'Art,' she corrected. 'Caricature, anyway. I used to have quite a flair for it myself, believe it or not,' she shyly admitted, 'before being a wife and mother took up most of my—time.'

Oh, damn. Her heart sank to her feet when she realised what she had just said. Zac Callum believed her and Daniel to be newly-weds; now he was frowning at her in confusion, and her teeth bit guiltily down on her full bottom lip at being caught out in the lie.

Luckily they were interrupted by someone who wanted to ask Zac questions. Deciding to take her chance and slip away while he was busy, and before she could drop herself and Daniel further in it, Rachel pushed her hands into her duffle coat pockets and turned to leave. But his hand coming out to catch her arm stopped her.

'Don't go,' he said. 'I need to say goodbye to the people who organised this, but if you'll wait for me, I would love your company for a drink in the pub I saw over the road.'

She hesitated as something close to temptation fizzed up inside her. Having a drink, in a pub, with a man who wasn't Daniel, constituted crossing that invisible line drawn by marriage. Or did it? she then asked herself defiantly. People did it all the time! Daniel did it all the time! The modern-day line was surely drawn much further down the page on morality. What harm could it do to anyone if she did accept? What business was it of anyone's if she did accept?

Daniel's business, she answered her own question. But ignored it. And ignored too the deep-seated knowledge that it was defiance making her ignore it. She liked Zac, she defended the temptation. She was interested in what he did.

'Thank you,' she heard herself accept. 'That would be nice.'

Funnily enough, he hesitated now, that shrewd speculative look she remembered from the first time she met him entering his eyes again.

Then he nodded and let go of her arm. 'Five minutes,' he promised, and walked away, leaving her standing there doing battle with whatever was niggling at her conscience.

Still, she enjoyed the hour they spent in the pub. The place was crowded because more than half the people who had been to the talk had crossed the road into it, and she and Zac stood leaning against two bar-stools with a glass of lager each.

It was nice, she decided, being here like this, being at ease and talked to as a reasonably intelligent human being rather than as a housewife or mother. She liked his relaxed manner, and the way he listened intently when—shyly at first, then with more enthusiasm when he didn't immediately shoot her down—she put her own ideas forward, surprising herself by what she had retained from her school days.

Daniel's name did not come into things until they were just about to part company, when Zac asked quietly, 'How long have you and Daniel been married, Rachel?'

She sighed, feeling the pleasure of the evening seep out of her. 'Seven years,' she answered, then, with a defiant lift of her small chin, 'We have three children. Two boys and a girl. And no, he doesn't keep me barefoot and pregnant. Sammy and Kate are twins.'

He smiled at the quip, but not with any humour. 'I think I owe you an apology for the first time we met,' he said.

He meant his references to Daniel's other women. Rachel felt an ache clench at her chest, but shrugged it and his apology away. 'No, you don't,' she answered.

'You were just being open and honest. It was Daniel and I who were being deceitful. Goodnight, Zac,' she added, before he could say anything else. She didn't want to talk about that night. She didn't want to know what else must be running through his mind right now. 'I enjoyed tonight very much. Thank you.'

Turning away, she went to unlock her car door when his voice stalled her. 'Listen,' he said. 'I'm thinking of doing a twelve-week course on Caricature here at this college one evening a week. Would you be interested in coming along to it?'

Would she? Rachel took her time turning back to face him, suspicious—well, half-suspicious—that he'd just thought of that on the spur of the moment.

Which meant—what exactly?

'I don't know,' she therefore answered warily. 'Is there enough interest here to make it worth your while?'

His cynical smile mocked her naïveté. He was, after all, a celebrity. People didn't need to be interested in what he did. Who he was would be enough to have them flocking to his class.

'You would enjoy it, Rachel,' he added softly when she said nothing. 'I can certainly promise you that.'

A small fizz of sensation erupted low down in her stomach, warning her that there was more to his promise than he was actually saying.

He was attracted to her. He had, in fact, made no effort to hide it.

The thing was, did she want to encourage something she knew had the potential to become very dangerous?

No, she answered herself flatly. Her life was complicated enough at the present without further complicating it with a man of Zac Callum's ilk.

Which was a shame, really, because if the man himself didn't appeal, the idea of taking up a sketch-pad and pencil again did.

'Let me know what you decide,' she prevaricated in the end, 'and I'll think about it.'

'Zac Callum teaching at a local art college?' Daniel was scornful to say the least. 'Why should he be bothered with small fry like that?'

'Maybe because he cares,' Rachel said, offended on Zac's behalf by Daniel's deriding tone.

He wasn't pleased that she'd gone out that night without his knowledge, but discovering that it was none other than Zac Callum who had tempted her out had turned him into a rather intriguingly surly brute!

'How did you know he was giving a talk?' he demanded.

'Local *Gazette*,' she replied. 'Have you eaten?' she asked, diplomatically changing the subject. 'Or do you want me to get you something?'

'No! I want to talk about you going out with Zac Callum!' he barked at her.

'I didn't go out with him!' she denied. 'I went to listen to him!' There was an ocean of difference between that and what Daniel was implying. 'What the hell are you trying to say, Daniel?' she demanded, beginning to lose patience. 'That we arranged some kind of elaborate set-up just so we could meet each other?'

The sudden flash of dark heat in his cheeks told her that that was exactly what he was thinking. 'He's capable of it,' he grunted. 'He fancied you from the first moment he laid eyes on you!'

My God, she thought, as an angry sense of elation whistled through her blood, the invincible Daniel Masterson was frightened that his little wife was considering taking on another man!

'It's you who is the untrustworthy person in this marriage, Daniel,' she reminded him bluntly. 'Not me.'

'But you could be out for revenge.'

'And you could be getting paranoid inside your guilty conscience,' she threw back. 'Don't tar me with the same brush as yourself.' And once again she deliberately ignored that little voice that was telling her she wasn't being entirely truthful.

'I wasn't doing that,' he sighed, going over to pour himself a stiff drink.

'Then what were you doing?' she snapped.

'Actually——' on another sigh, he shook his dark head wearily '—actually, I don't know what I'm doing,' he confessed. 'Are you going to take the course?'

'Are you going to play the domineering husband by telling me I can't if I decide I want to?' she countered, small chin coming up.

'Will you listen to me if I do try to talk you out of it?' he parried drily.

'No.'

He shrugged. 'Then it isn't worth my trying, is it?' he said, and walked out of the room, leaving her sitting there feeling angry and frustrated and a hundred other things that revolved almost entirely around one emotion. Hurt. Whether she fought with him or made love with him or simply ignored his very existence, she still hurt like a love-lost child whenever he walked away from her.

The trouble with you, Rachel, is you've gone so long living for him, you have no idea how to live for yourself!

Which was why she decided to go on the course when Zac rang to tell her it was all set up.

Daniel didn't say a word—not a single word. But, good grief, she knew his opinion by the time she left the house for her first class a couple of weeks later. And when she came back he didn't wait for the darkness to shroud their marriage-bed before he reached for her. He grabbed her hand almost as soon as she walked through the door and hauled her up to bed, staking claim over her senses in

a way that left them both bitterly frustrated, because
even while she went eagerly with him through the blistering avenues of sensuality, he still reached heaven alone.

Which, in the end, satisfied neither of them.

But at least her flair for caricature blossomed through
the ensuing weeks. And even Daniel had to smile at the
fun she made of them all with her pencil.

Zac was quietly encouraging. It helped that he never
made any personal reference during the classes themselves but later, when they all retired to the pub across
the road for a drink before going home, he would always
make sure he sat next to her, his interest in her more
than clear then. She tried to ignore it most of the time,
wanting to learn all he had to teach her about drawing
and frightened that, if he came on too strong with her,
she would have to give it all up.

December loomed on the horizon: Rachel became engrossed in Christmas preparations. Shopping, planning,
mad bursts of cooking and baking that filled the freezer
to its limits and made everyone's mouth water as the
different rich and spicy smells permeated the house.

Daniel became even busier—and more preoccupied.
His one real concession to Rachel's restless need to be
seen as an individual in her own right was to take her
out on a regular basis. They went to the theatre, the
cinema, to clubs and restaurants. Her wardrobe, by
necessity, became filled with yet more elegant clothes,
although she'd soon returned to wearing her casual stuff
for the more mundane areas of her life. But she kept the
new hairstyle because she liked it, and she found it easier
to manage than the long, thick swath she used to have.

But the strain their marriage was putting on her began
to tell in other ways. She tired easily, became fractious
over the silliest things, and would burst into fits of
weeping for no apparent reason, which troubled her

family and made them yearn for the other sunnier Rachel they used to know.

Growing pains, she ruefully diagnosed her problem, after one such uncalled-for outburst had the children creeping around her warily and Daniel studying her through those hooded eyes which rarely looked directly at her these days.

Her car wouldn't start one evening when she was about to go to her evening class. Daniel was in Huddersfield and not expected back until very late that night. Jenny was baby-sitting. It was sleeting heavily outside, and Rachel looked reluctantly towards the house she had just left, knowing she should go back inside and call a taxi but oddly unwilling to do so now she had escaped.

Escaped! It hit her, then, that she was beginning to see her home as some kind of emotional prison.

On a heavy sigh, she pulled her warm coat up around her ears and walked off down the drive to catch the bus.

She arrived at the centre soaked through to her skin, her hair plastered to her head and her face white with cold. The rotten weather had found its way right through to her clothes beneath and, on a mass cry of concern, the class set about helping her to get dry. Someone began rubbing at her hair with a paper towel while someone else pulled off her boots and wet woollen socks.

'Socks!' someone cried in mock horror. 'The lady wears men's woolly socks inside her dainty boots!'

Everyone laughed, and so did Rachel, light-hearted and suddenly feeling set free from something she had been dragging around with her for weeks now. Her blouse was wet, and Zac pulled off his own black woollen sweater for her to use. She took off her blouse and put it on while the other women in the class shielded her from interested male eyes.

By the time they had all finished with her her wet clothes lay across the warm radiators drying, and she was dressed in nothing more than her underwear beneath Zac's big sweater which came down to her knees.

But her clothes were still very damp when it was time to leave, and swapping the warm sweater for her damp shirt and jeans gave her no pleasure. When Zac offered to give her a lift straight home, instead of going with the rest of them to the local pub, Rachel read the expression in his eyes but accepted anyway, stubbornly ignoring what the warning bells going off in her head were telling her.

He drove a new model Porsche which gripped the icy wet road like glue and surged off with a growling show of power. 'Mmm,' she murmured luxuriously as the car's heater began to warm her cold legs.

Zac glanced at her and smiled. She had her eyes closed, a contented smile playing about her mouth. 'Better?' he asked.

'Mmm,' she murmured again. 'Sorry you had to miss your pint.'

'No bother,' he dismissed, then added softly, 'I'd rather be here with you.'

Rachel's eyes flicked open, a warning *frisson* skipping down her spine. 'Next left,' she directed.

Dutifully, he made the turn. 'What does Daniel think of your being with me every Wednesday night?' he enquired smoothly then.

Rachel shrugged. She didn't want to talk about Daniel—she didn't want to hoist up her guard either. 'He's very encouraging,' she said, then grimaced at the lie. Daniel hated it and, because he hated it, she rubbed his nose in it. He rarely saw her without a sketch-pad in her hands these days—reminding him of who had helped her rediscover her love of drawing.

'Yet you never draw him, do you?' Zac prodded quietly. 'You poke fun at every other member of your family, but never him.'

'He isn't a good subject,' she said. 'Go right at the next junction.'

'Daniel?' His tone was filled with mockery. 'I would have thought him an ideal subject, being the hard-hitting, ruthless devil he is at work and the ordinary family man he is at home. Real scope for humour there by mixing the two, I would say.'

But Rachel didn't agree. She saw nothing funny in Daniel any more. Once, maybe, she would have delighted in drawing him in cartoon form. But not any more. 'Then maybe I'll have a go one day,' she said lightly, knowing she would not. 'This is it,' she told him. 'The white rendered one with the black BMW parked outside.'

So Daniel was home. She shivered slightly, but not with the cold.

Zac drew the car to a halt at the bottom of the drive. The engine died, and they both sat there listening to the rain thunder against the glass. He turned in his seat to look at her, and Rachel made herself return the look.

'Well—thank you for the lift,' she said, without making a single move to get out of the car. She felt trapped, by Zac's expression, by the warmth inside the car, by her own breathlessness caused by the darkened look in his eyes.

'My pleasure,' he said, but absently. His mind was elsewhere, searching her face for something she wasn't sure whether she was showing him or not. Then she found she was, because he leaned across the gap separating them and kissed her gently on the mouth. She didn't respond, but nor did she pull away. Her heart gave a small leap, then began thundering in her breast, but she wasn't certain whether that was because she was playing with fire here, or because she was genuinely attracted to him.

His hand covered her cheek, long artistic fingers running into her hair, and as the kiss continued he moved his thumb until it rested against the corner of her mouth and began stroking gently, urging it to respond.

But even as he did so she was pulling away, suddenly very sure that this was not what she wanted to do. He let her go, sitting back to study her through lazy, glittering eyes.

'I'm sorry,' she mumbled awkwardly—why, she wasn't sure.

'What for?'

She didn't answer—couldn't. All she wanted to do now was to get out of this car. And her hand fumbled for the door-catch again, trembling in its urgency to get away.

'You wanted me to kiss you, Rachel,' Zac murmured softly. 'Whatever else is going through your mind right now, remember you wanted it as much as I did.'

He was right, and her cheeks flushed with guilt. She had wanted him to kiss her—had wanted to know what it was like to feel another man's lips besides Daniel's against her own.

But now she just felt foolish, and angry with herself for allowing it to happen, because it had encouraged Zac to think there might be a place for him in her life, when there never could be. Daniel was everything she wanted, damn him. Damn him to hell.

It was only as she ran through the driving rain towards the house that she wondered suddenly if Daniel had heard them arrive. She sent a sharp glance at the curtained windows, but there was no revealing twitching of velvet. He hadn't seen her kissing Zac, she decided with relief. He would be expecting her to come home by bus, so even if he'd heard the car, he would not have associated the deep sound of Zac's Porsche with her arrival home.

He wasn't in the sitting-room. The study door was ajar and she glanced in but there was no sign of him there either. She found him in the kitchen.

'You're back earlier than I expected,' she remarked casually as she entered. He had his back to her as he waited for the kettle to boil. And he looked nice in a simple black sweatshirt and casual jeans.

'I let my mother go home,' he told her, ignoring her remark. His hand was shaking a little as he poured the boiling water on to the tea-bags. 'She was concerned about you when she saw your car was still on the drive and you were nowhere to be found. You could have let her know that you weren't taking your own car.'

'It wouldn't start,' she explained. 'So I caught the bus. I'm sorry,' she added belatedly. 'I didn't think it would worry Jenny. I'll apologise to her tomorrow...'

Silence. He still hadn't looked at her, his whole attention seemingly fixed on the tea-tray he was preparing. It suddenly hit her that Daniel was blindingly angry about something. It showed in the cording of the muscles in his neck, in the way his every movement was being severely controlled as he moved about the kitchen without so much as glancing her way.

Had he seen? Letting out a nervous little laugh, she said, 'I'm soaking wet through!' Trying to sound normal and failing miserably, guilt was staining her cheeks red. And she knew that if Daniel did bother to look at her he would know in an instant that she had been up to no good. 'I think I'll go and have a hot bath,' she decided nervously. Then, belatedly, 'H-Have you eaten? Can I get you anything before I——'

'*No*!' he barked out so violently that Rachel jumped.

Chewing pensively on her lower lip, she watched him make an effort to control himself, his shoulders heaving on a long intake of air as he lifted his face from its con-

templation of the teapot to stare at the slatted blinds
covering the kitchen window.

'No,' he repeated more levelly. 'I've already eaten.
Thank you.'

'Then I'll...' She floundered to a halt, staring help-
lessly at the uncommunicative length of his rigid back—
then fled.

He had seen, she accepted uneasily as she watched the
water fill the bath, and felt a skitter of alarm chase down
her spine, but could not make up her mind whether it
was caused by fear, guilt or just the sheer thrill of getting
her own back if only in a small way.

She went to bed feeling tense with nervous anticipation, a driving defiance, and ready to do battle when
Daniel eventually joined her.

But he didn't join her. Daniel did not come to bed at
all that night.

# CHAPTER EIGHT

THE next few weeks were horrible. Daniel turned into a grim-faced uncommunicative stranger, and their nights were cold, dark places where he did not so much as touch her. The children became fractious—excited about the coming Christmas, Rachel blamed, but really she knew that it was her and Daniel's fault. The strain in their marriage was affecting the children almost as badly as it was affecting them.

The trouble was that she didn't know what to do about it, short of going to Daniel and making a full confession of what had gone on between herself and Zac, before humbly asking for his forgiveness, and she couldn't do that. It smacked too much of caring what he thought or felt, and she was determined not to care—outwardly anyway.

Then one day Rachel was sick. She spent the whole day wandering aimlessly around the house, feeling dull-witted and weak-tummied, and the twins had to pick that same evening after school to play noisily about the house until her head was thumping like a sledge-hammer, and she was plainly relieved when Daniel walked through the front door so that she could pass responsibility over to him and drag herself off to bed.

'Why didn't you call me?' he rebuked as he watched her slog her way up the stairs. 'I would have come home straight away if you'd only let me know you didn't feel well!'

She just shrugged an obscure reply and continued on. It had not even entered her head to call him. In fact, she realised as she crawled beneath the duvet, she had never rung him at work—not in all the years since they married. Daniel called home often enough, but she'd never bothered to call him. And again she was struck by that invisible barrier they'd managed to erect between Daniel the husband and father and Daniel the high-powered businessman. And she could not bring to mind one single time when she had voluntarily crossed that barrier.

Well, whatever he was at this moment, she noted as she settled with relief into the blessed darkness, he had effectively quietened the children, and within seconds she had fallen into a blissful sleep which remained that way because not a single sound in the house was allowed to disturb her.

She came awake long hours later to find it was already morning and that Daniel was standing over her. 'I thought you might want this...' He was standing with a mug of something hot in his hand. As he spoke, he put it down on the bedside table. 'How are you feeling this morning?' he enquired coolly.

'Better,' she said, though she was very careful not to jolt her tender stomach as she levered her way up the pillows, then pushed her hair away from her pale face before reaching for the mug. 'Thank you,' she murmured.

Daniel hovered, studying her grimly. 'I can take the day off,' he offered. 'Work from home if you want.'

Rachel shook her head. 'It's not necessary,' she assured him. 'I'll probably feel a bit weak today, but I can manage OK.'

'Still...' It was odd, but she got the distinct impression he was struggling with something. 'You'd better not plan on going to your class tonight—not while you're feeling so under the weather...'

The mug of tea was hot. She blew absently at the steam. 'We've planned a Christmas party tonight,' she informed him as lightly as she could manage. 'Zac is taking us all out to a club after class. I don't want to miss it.'

Her tone smacked of the usual defiance, and from the corner of her vision she saw his jaw twitch revealingly. He was trying hard not to make the cutting remark she just knew was hanging on the end of his tongue. It was horrible; even while she wanted to taunt him, it was horrible.

'We'll see how you feel later,' was all he eventually replied, then turned to leave.

And suddenly she felt an aching need to make him stay! 'M-My parents are coming down for Christmas as usual,' she rushed out, watching him halt stiffly by the bedroom door. 'But we have a problem this year...' He didn't look at her, just waited for her to say what the problem was with his back placed firmly towards her. 'Last year we didn't have Michael taking up the spare bedroom. Now I don't know how we're going to put them up for two nights—I just can't imagine my father jammed between two chairs in your study while my mother hogs the sofa in the sitting-room!' She'd meant it as a joke but, as Daniel turned to look at her, she saw he was not smiling and felt her heart sink even deeper into that cold, bleak place where it existed these days.

'So what do you want me to do about it?' he demanded. 'I've lost count of the times I've tried to get you to move to something bigger than this house. But you would never so much as discuss it. Well, now you're stuck with a problem that you will just have to solve on your own, because I'm damned if I'm having anything to do with it!'

Rachel stared at him in angry amazement as he just turned and slammed out of the room.

\* \* \*

She went to her evening class that night. Not because she felt well enough to go—because she didn't. And not because she wanted to go—which she didn't. But because she felt so angry with Daniel that she refused to give him the satisfaction he would feel if she stayed at home instead!

But she did not enjoy it. Her mind was preoccupied with a million and one things she could be doing at home, and her stomach refused to settle down. She was tired, tense and pale. And, on top of all that, Zac spent the whole time watching her through dark, disturbing eyes.

OK, so it was the first time since he first met her that he'd seen her in anything but jeans, and she had to acknowledge that he looked rather dishy himself in a dark silk lounge suit and creamy shirt. She was wearing a little black dress she had bought on that first bout of restlessness that had sent her up to London to create her new image. It was off-the-shoulder, short and figure-hugging, and she received several teasingly provocative comments from some of the other men when they saw her.

But the way Zac was looking at her made her feel distinctly uncomfortable. And his eyes kept on telling her that he was remembering that kiss they'd started in his car, whereas Rachel had spent the last few weeks trying to dismiss it from her mind. Which wasn't difficult—it was the guilt that was the hardest to dismiss, not the kiss.

They were going on to a local nightclub later. It was in actual fact an old cinema converted into a club. They'd booked a table in the mezzanine restaurant that looked down on the old stalls area, which was now a disco dance-floor with laser lights and throbbing disco music played so loud that it was virtually impossible to speak. Any other time she would have thoroughly enjoyed the whole thing. The places Daniel took her to were more sophisticated and sedate, the restaurants quiet, the music easy-listening, middle-of-the-road stuff. And until this last bust-up with him she had been quite looking forward simply to letting her hair down and discoing the night away.

As it was, her stomach would not let her enjoy the meal she'd ordered, and the music grated on her thumping head. Zac had pulled his chair up close to hers and was insisting on monopolising her attention with soft conversation that forced her to lean towards him to catch what he was saying, and brought her into too intimate contact with his body.

Then he began touching her—nothing too heavy, just light brushes of his long fingers against her arm, her shoulder, her cheek and her hair. But she became so uptight with the situation, and felt so helpless to know what to do about it without causing a scene in front of the others, that she was glad when he suddenly asked her to dance.

At least dancing meant no body contact—not the kind of dancing they did here anyway—so she let him lead her down the stairs on to the dance-floor, then almost groaned when, determinedly, he pulled her into his arms.

'No, Zac,' she objected, trying to move away from him.

'Don't be stupid, Rachel,' he drawled. 'It's only a dance.'

No, it wasn't, and he knew it. After weeks of playing it relatively cool, he had decided to make his move on her. And if she didn't put a stop to him now, then she really would be guilty of betraying Daniel.

'No,' she repeated firmly, slapped his hands away and turned to walk off the floor.

She shouldn't have come. She had known she shouldn't have come after that kiss they'd shared in his car. She'd known from the moment their eyes clashed across the lecture hall weeks ago that she should not have anything to do with Zac.

He wanted her and she did not want him.

She wanted Daniel. Only Daniel. And that hurt so much that it made her want to weep inside.

She sensed Zac behind her as she made her way to the main foyer, but refused to look back at him as she moved grimly for the line of phone booths and began ringing the several different taxi companies whose telephone numbers were scrawled all over the pay-phone backboard.

But to no avail. It was Christmas, and anyone with any sense had booked their ride home before even coming out.

In sheer desperation she rang home, her stomach flipping wistfully when Daniel's deep voice came impatiently down the line.

'It's me,' she murmured huskily.

There was a long pause on the other end, where all she could hear was Daniel's steady breathing whispering in her ear. 'What's the matter?' he asked at last.

'I—can't get home,' she confessed. 'I've tried all the taxi firms and they're all booked out... What shall I do?'

Just like that. As easily as that she had fallen back into her old Rachel role. Any problem, refer it to Daniel. He would deal with it. He would sort it out. And all she had to do was stand back and wait for a solution to come via the man who had never let her down yet. Not in this way anyway.

There followed another silence, and Rachel lowered her head, hugging the dark grey plastic receiver to her ear, as though by doing so she was hugging tightly to Daniel himself.

'Won't your—Romeo bring you?' he taunted eventually.

'He's not my Romeo!' she denied. 'And—anyway,' she added, 'I . . .' No, she changed her mind about what she had been going to say, not wanting to give Daniel the pleasure of hearing that she did not want Zac anywhere near her. 'I can't drag him away from a good party so early just because I've had enough—can't you come for me, Daniel?' she pleaded softly.

'What about the children?' he came back sarcastically. 'Am I supposed to leave them here on their own while I come out to get you?'

'Oh.' She felt foolish again. She hadn't considered that problem. All she had done was realise she was in a mess and ring the man who always put things right for her.

'Now she wishes she had taken my advice and employed a nanny!' he mocked her acidly.

'I'll get Zac to bring me,' she hit right back. The nanny thing was an old point of friction between them. Daniel wanted a bigger house, a housekeeper to take care of it, a nanny to take care of the children. What Rachel would like to know was what was left for her to do if he made her redundant in just about every part she played in his life.

'I'll call my mother, get her over here to sit while I come and get you.' Daniel changed tack like a sailor, his voice like a rattlesnake waving its tail in warning. 'I'll have to get her out of bed, I suppose, and she won't like it—for which I don't blame her. But I'll——'

'Oh—no,' Rachel drawled in angry refusal. 'I wouldn't like to think that I had inconvenienced you all to that extent. Zac will do it just as easily!' And she slammed down the phone before Daniel could come back with a reply.

'No luck?' She turned to find Zac leaning against the wall, not three feet away from her, his eyes flickering curiously over her angry red cheeks. She had no idea how much of her conversation with Daniel he had over-heard, and at that precise moment didn't care.

'No,' she clipped. 'I'll just have to call one of the taxi firms back and book the next car they have free.' Her shrug told him she was already resigning herself to a long wait.

'I'll take you,' he offered. Rachel stared at him dubiously. She did not feel like half an hour more of his company. But then neither did she feel like hanging around here for the hour or so the taxi companies had said she would have to wait. Zac made the decision for her, reaching out to take hold of her wrist. 'Come on,' he said quietly. 'I'll take you—I'll take you, Rachel.'

His green eyes mocked her foolishness. And, tired, fed up and feeling more than a little depressed by the constant emotional battle she seemed to be having with everyone around her, including herself, she gave in.

They went together to retrieve her coat, then braved the biting December wind outside to scramble inside the bright red Porsche. Then they were driving out of the club's car park and on to the main road while she huddled into her thick woollen coat, watching emptily as the salt-stained road slid slickly beneath them.

'Why do you put up with him when he's such a selfish bastard?' Zac bit out suddenly.

'Aren't all men?' she countered tartly.

'Not like Daniel,' he muttered. 'I still find it hard to believe that he's married to someone like you.' He glanced at her. 'The Lydia Marsdens of this world suit him much better, you know.'

It was a ruthless thrust and hit home painfully, draining her lungs and blanching her face, because she couldn't even argue the point with him. Lydia Marsden *was* probably more suited to Daniel—not that she'd ever seen the woman to judge—not that she ever wanted to see her.

Lydia Marsden was the faceless ghost who visited her in the night. That wretched haunting was more than enough to deal with.

'And Mandy Sales,' he added tauntingly. 'That was quite a revealing confrontation you all had on the dance-floor that night, wasn't it?'

'You overheard?' Rachel gasped.

'Half the room overheard it, darling,' he drawled. 'And stood in stunned amazement as it all began to sink in. Daniel Masterson——' his smile was drily mocking '—whiz-kid of the new-age tycoons, had a little wife and three children tucked away nobody seemed to know about— I bet that news, when it got out, hit Lydia right where it hurts the most. She was after marrying him, you know. Daniel was the ideal choice for an up-and-coming corporate lawyer like her.'

So Lydia was a lawyer, not Daniel's secretary, as she had assumed. The news jolted her. Compete with that if you can, she mocked herself bitterly. It was one thing believing you were fighting an ordinary secretary for your husband's attention—but some female hot-shot lawyer?

As if thinking along similar lines, Zac murmured curiously, 'If you've been married for seven years, then that means you caught him before Daniel made his meteoric elevation into the killing-fields of finance. So what does that make you, Rachel?' he asked. 'A hanger-on from his reckless youth?'

Insults were insults and, in Rachel's mind, some were probably deserved. But that last remark had aimed to cut—and cut it had, if only because it pierced directly at the truth she was beginning to believe for herself.

'I think you'd better shut up and stop this car so I can get out before you say something I'll take real exception to,' she snapped.

To her consternation he did exactly that, pulling the car into the kerb and stopping with a jerk before turning to glare angrily at her. 'Well, I've already taken exception,' he muttered, 'to the way you've been playing me along all these weeks. My God!' he grated before she could say anything. 'I never stood a chance with you, did I?'

'No,' she answered honestly.

'Then why the hell didn't you stop me before we got in this deep?'

'This deep—what deep?' She turned to challenge him with a deriding look. 'We haven't done anything but share a fumbled kiss on a rainy night!'

'We were sharing more than that, Rachel, and you know it,' he scathed her derision. 'But it was all just a game with you, wasn't it? You saw I fancied you and thought you would play me along for a while. What was it?' he demanded bitterly. 'Did your ego need a bit of a lift? Has it begun to get to you at last that he gets a bigger kick out of bedding his legal adviser than he does his wife?'

She hit him then, her hand striking at his cheek while her own face went white with pain. Then she made a grab for the door-handle, her other hand fumbling to unfasten her seatbelt so that she could get away. But Zac grabbed her arm, his fingers biting. 'Oh, no,' he muttered. 'You don't get away with that so easily.'

With a tug he pulled her against him, and his mouth came down on top of hers. It was an intrusion—a vile rape of her unresponsive mouth. And by the time he let her go again she was choking on the taste of him.

Then thankfully she was out of the car, slamming the door shut in his hard angry face.

He didn't hang around. He fired the car engine into life, then was driving off on a screech of tyres, leaving her standing there in the biting cold wind, watching his red tail-lights disappear from view.

She dragged a hand across her mouth, grimacing when she felt the telling sting which said he had managed to cut her inner lip. Damn him! she thought, wishing herself back in that old fairy-tale world she used to exist in, where nothing nasty happened. Damn Mandy for waking her up out of it! she added bitterly as she began the walk home. Damn Daniel for his infidelity and damn Lydia for giving in to his expert seduction! But most of all—damn herself!

She wasn't too far away from home, she noted thankfully, but her feet were killing her by the time she hobbled through the front door, and she kicked the offending high heels off as soon as she'd closed the door behind her. It was warm inside, after the biting cold night air.

One o'clock, she noticed testily as she climbed the stairs. She felt utterly done in; depression sat on the top of her head with a vengeance and the ugly scene with Zac echoed over and over in her mind. She didn't bother trying to look for Daniel. He could be in hell for all she cared. And anyway, she was in no mood for yet another row tonight. He obviously agreed that they'd done enough of that on the phone because he hadn't bothered meeting her with the proverbial whip at the front door as she came in.

But she was wrong if she thought he was going to ignore her completely. She had only managed to strip off her dress and pull on her dressing-gown when he entered the bedroom, her discarded shoes dangling from his fingers.

'You forgot these.' He dropped them by the closed bedroom door.

'I didn't forget them,' she snapped. 'I just left them where they came off.' She was sitting on the edge of the bed, massaging her aching toes, her head lowered so that the soft cloud of her hair hid her face from view.

'He didn't bring you all the way home,' he remarked with suspicious levity.

Been spying through cracks in the curtains again? she wondered bitterly. 'Maybe he didn't bring me at all,' was all she said.

'You haven't had time to walk all that way.'

I've walked far enough! she thought, studying her poor aching feet.

'Have a lovers' tiff, did you?' He was getting nasty; she could hear the level of control dropping with each word.

'Something like that,' she shrugged, getting off the bed and walking towards the bathroom. Let him think what he liked! she thought mutinously. Let him think what he damned well liked.

His hands grasping hold of her upper arms brought her spinning round to face him. He wasn't just angry, she noted on a small bubble of alarm, he was furious— tense with it, pulsing with it, eyes like silver beacons.

'And what was this—tiff about?' he demanded tightly. 'Wouldn't you go back to his place with him? Is that it? What's the matter, Rachel—weren't you in the mood?'

Her own eyes flashed, bitterness and a downright disgust with men in general tonight making her retaliate in kind. 'But how do you know I haven't been at his place all evening?' she taunted. 'I could have rung you just as easily from there, you know. How are you to know the difference?'

He went white, his fingers biting painfully into her flesh, hard eyes flashing over her face as if he were looking for evidence to prove what she was suggesting could be true. 'Your lip,' he growled. 'He bruised your lip!'

'And you're bruising my arms!' she cried. 'Will you let go?' She tried to pull away but he just increased his grip until she winced.

'How could you?' he bit out hoarsely. 'How could you do it, Rachel? How could you?'

It was all beginning to boil. It had been threatening to do it for long enough, and at last the full force of their pent-up emotions was beginning to bubble to the surface.

'I tell you what, Daniel,' she flashed, 'let's exchange notes since you're so damned interested! You tell me how it was with Lydia and I'll tell you how it was with Zac!'

'God, stop it!' He closed his eyes, pain raking across his features, and Rachel felt tears of utter wretchedness burn at the back of her eyes. For the second time that night she hit out at a man, hitting him with both her fists until Daniel let her go.

'You disgust me, do you know that?' she whispered bitterly, and flung herself into the bathroom, her fingers trembling as she slid home the small bolt which was never used.

When she came out again, calmer but by no means under control, she found Daniel sitting on the bed with his head buried in his hands. It hurt to see him like that. But, there again, everything hurt these days. She couldn't remember a time when she had last felt like laughing in this house.

'I want to go to bed,' she said, refusing point-blank to give in to those weaker feelings his defeated pose raked her with.

He didn't move, and after a long taut minute while she stood there, hovering between a bitter desire to hit him again and a weak need to run over there and hold him, simply hold him because he was hurting and she loved him—damn her!—loved him no matter what he said or did to her—she felt something go snap inside her, and on a groan that was a wretched cry of frustration she dropped down on her knees in front of him, her hands going up to grasp his wrists angrily, pulling them away from his face.

'Do you really want to know what happened tonight?' she demanded shrilly. 'He came on to me but I repulsed him, so he paid me back by taunting me with Lydia!' The hurt shot across her eyes and Daniel closed his to shut it out. 'Lydia,' she repeated thickly. 'The high-powered lawyer who is far more Daniel Masterson's type than pathetic little Rachel is!'

'That's not true,' he whispered tensely.

'No?' Tears spread across her eyes, the torture of it all making her heart muscles tremble. 'Well, I think it's true,' she asserted thickly. 'We've grown apart, Daniel! You going one way while I've stayed still, and I think the Lydia Marsdens of this world are far more your type now!'

To her surprise, he laughed, deridingly shaking his dark head as if he couldn't believe she'd actually said that. 'Does it look as though I've grown apart from you?' he demanded tightly. 'Am I straining at the leash to get away? Are my suitcases packed and standing by the door? Hard ruthless bastard that I am, Rachel, don't you think I'm quite capable of walking away from you if I decided it was what I wanted to do?' She had no idea how it happened, but suddenly it was Daniel gripping her wrists, not the other way around.

She shook her head. 'Lydia,' she murmured. 'She's——'

'To hell with bloody Lydia,' he dismissed scathingly. 'This is not about her. This is about you and me and whether we can still stand the sight of each other!'

'Guilty conscience, then!' she sighed. 'You stay because of your damned guilty conscience!'

'Well, I certainly have one of those!' he bitterly agreed. 'But don't be foolish enough to grant me concessions where none are due,' he warned. 'I am no one's martyr,

Rachel. If I believed this marriage of ours a waste of time, I would have walked out long ago. Be sure of it. This is the nineteen-nineties after all,' he added cynically. 'Marriages break up all the time. No,' he murmured roughly, 'this is why I stay.' He pulled her towards him to kiss her hard. 'I want you,' he growled. 'I can't honestly get enough of you! Even after seven years I can still get hot in the groin just looking at you! My God!' he added harshly. 'I can't even stop myself from taking you when I know I can no longer satisfy you.'

He shook his dark head in self-disgust. 'But that doesn't explain why you haven't thrown me out,' he went on grimly. 'How can you, Rachel, having had me hurt you, break your trust, make your life a misery? Why?' He gave her wrists a hard shake. 'Why haven't you told me to get out?'

'I...' No. She shook her head, refusing to answer, because the answer was so utterly degrading to her already humiliated soul.

'Then would you *like* to call it a day?' He altered the challenge slightly. 'And have me out of your life?'

Her body jerked in reaction, a harsh stab of pain cutting right through her. 'No,' she whispered, feeling the weighted beginning of tears build in her chest.

'Why not?' he persisted ruthlessly. 'How do you stand having me living in the same house with you—sleeping in the same bed as you—touching you—holding you—how do you stand it, Rachel? How—how—how?'

Because I love you, you rotten bastard! she thought, and let the tears break free on a helpless sob.

Daniel sighed, the sound coming from some deeply wretched part of him, and the next thing she knew he had freed her captured wrists to wrap his arms around her and he was falling back, taking her with him, his body covering her, curling around her and holding her, holding her so tight and so close she could barely breathe.

'Does this feel as though we've grown apart?' he demanded sensually.

'No.' This felt wonderful, the only place in the world she wanted to be.

'Then shut up about us growing apart,' he said thickly, then kissed her, long and fiercely, giving her no chance to think, no chance to recover, but just governing her every thought and feeling until she began to sink languidly into the warm morass of his loving.

'Did you let that bastard touch you, Rachel?' The rough-voiced enquiry brought her swimming protestingly up from the wonderful place she had sunk to.

Her eyes flicked open, furious blue staring into tortured grey, searching, half refusing to believe that he had actually asked her that question.

But he had. 'Did you?' he persisted when she said nothing. 'I want to know—I *need* to know! God,' he choked, 'I *have to know*!'

She stared at him for a moment longer, then bared her angry teeth to say, 'Go to hell.'

He did, it seemed, she realised later, go straight to hell, but he made sure he took her with him. It happened with an angry passion that had him wrenching open her robe then releasing himself from his own clothes so he could thrust inside her with such appalling ruthlessness that she didn't think she took a single breath until it was all over.

Then she rolled away on to her own side of the bed and Daniel went into the bathroom and shut the door.

He stayed in there a long time. Long enough to let her crawl beneath the duvet and be asleep by the time he came back.

The next evening, the telephone began ringing just as she was clearing away the children's evening meal. She walked towards the hall extension and picked it up, frowning in annoyance because the children had the TV on too loud.

'Rachel Masterson,' she murmured absently into the receiver, stretching the telephone cable to its limits in her effort to reach the sitting-room door so that she could pull it to.

There was a pause on the other end of the line, then a cool voice asked to speak to Daniel.

'I'm afraid he isn't home yet,' she answered. 'Can I take a message or get him to call you back?'

Another pause while the caller deliberated with herself, and Rachel looked distractedly at the time. She had a pair of steaks under the grill; if the woman didn't hurry up, she——

'This is Lydia Marsden,' the cool voice explained, and Rachel went absolutely still.

# CHAPTER NINE

RACHEL was still staring at the telephone where she had placed it very carefully back on its rest when Daniel came home a few moments later. He saw her as soon as he got in the door—and stopped dead in his tracks.

'What is it?' he asked sharply, seeing at a glance that she was suffering some kind of shock.

Her hand lifted to her cheek, ice-cold fingers resting on equally cold flesh. 'Lydia just called,' she told him blankly. 'She wants you to call her back.'

As she continued to stare at him, wondering if she was just going to faint quietly away or go the whole hog and fall apart at the very seams, she saw Daniel's face suffuse with hot colour, watched his chest lift and fall on a single throbbing breath as emotion, the like of which she had never seen him display before, threatened to explode right over her bemused head.

His mouth tightened and lost all vestige of colour, his nostrils flaring like a wild animal threatening attack. He dropped his briefcase to the floor, sucking in another breath through teeth so tightly clenched that the air whistled as it was pulled into his heaving lungs.

Then he moved to a paralysed Rachel, taking hold of her to move her bodily out of the way so that he could get to his study. The door slammed shut behind him. Rachel stood staring at it, wondering just what had taken place here in her hallway—besides the holocaust happening inside herself, that was.

132

The mere mention of Lydia's name could bring on a reaction like that? Have him bodily shifting her aside like that?

She choked on a strangled sob, then quite ruthlessly controlled herself, refusing to give in to what was going on inside her.

Lydia had called, and Daniel had run like a man possessed!

She was nursing Michael in the sitting-room when Daniel came looking for her. He looked pale, and, although most of that terrible emotion had diminished, she could still see the residue glimmering in his eyes. Kate ran to him for her customary hug but only received a token stroke of her golden head. Sam waved a leg— he was stretched out in front of the TV, engrossed in an old black and white movie. Michael was tired, and only fit to give his father a concessionary glance before sinking himself back into the pleasure of being held in his mother's arms.

Daniel was looking fixedly at Rachel. 'I apologise,' he said roughly. 'She's been told never to ring here.'

'It doesn't matter.'

'Of course it bloody matters!' he barked, and in unison the children turned to stare at him in surprise. He ran an impatient hand through his hair, sighing in an effort to control himself. 'Sammy—Kate. Play with Michael for a moment while I talk to your mother.'

Without waiting for any arguments, he plucked a complaining Michael out of Rachel's arms and sat him between Sam's legs on the floor, gathered together a se-lection of toys around them, then smiled at all three in what Rachel assumed to be an attempt at reassurance since they were all staring warily at him.

Then he turned and grasped Rachel's hand, pulling her to her feet and through to his study, only letting go of her when they were safely shut behind the closed door.

'She's been told never to call here,' he repeated tautly. 'She was told to get the damned cleaner to call me if it was that urgent! But never to do it herself!'

'As I said, it doesn't matter.'

'But it does matter!' he exploded with rasping ferocity. 'She hurt you just now—and I was determined that was not going to happen!'

'Then you should have...' She bit back the accusing words wanting to tumble from her lips and, with a small shrug, moved jerkily to his desk, finding his scattered papers in sudden need of tidying. 'How is it that she still works for you?' she questioned tightly. 'If you say it's over.' It had been a bitter blow that, finding out that Lydia still worked for him.

'She doesn't work for me,' he said tightly. 'She works for the firm of lawyers I employ,' he explained at her puzzled look. 'I had all my business transferred to one of her partners weeks ago.'

She didn't believe him. She could still see the expression on his face when she had told him Lydia rang. She could still feel the way he had moved her roughly to one side.

She shuddered. 'Then what is she doing calling here?' she asked.

Daniel took in a short breath, still struggling, she was sure, with the emotions Lydia's call caused to erupt. 'She happened to be the last in their suite of offices when some urgent information came through by fax,' he explained. 'It was important enough to necessitate someone informing me as soon as possible. And she was the only person there to do it!'

'Oh.' That was all Rachel could think of to say to that. 'Well, just make sure she never calls here again,' she added flatly, and in a tone which decidedly closed the subject.

But the uncomfortable silence that followed warned her there was more to come.

She was right. 'The thing is,' he began carefully, 'it means I have to go out again, almost immediately. A legal problem has developed with the Huddersfield take-over and I have to go back to the office to sort it out personally.'

The Harvey take-over, the Huddersfield take-over—what was the difference? 'Of course you do,' she agreed, with such acid understanding that it was like a slap in the face. 'And I have to put the children to bed.'

Pushing past him, she went to leave the room.

But Daniel stopped her. 'No.' Grabbing hold of her, he brought her to stand in front of him. 'I'm going to my own office, Rachel.' His eyes were a cool, steady, honest grey. 'Not Lydia's office. She has already faxed me the information I need—to my own office,' he emphasised clearly. 'I won't see her. I don't want to see her. We will have the full width of London between us—do you understand?'

Understand? Yes, she understood. He was demanding she trust his word. His steady gaze was insisting she trust his word.

A trust she did not feel she could give him.

Could maybe never give him again.

'Michael needs me,' she murmured, and pulled free to leave the room.

That had been Friday. On Monday he was going up to Huddersfield to tie up the loose ends of the deal before the Christmas break. And after an awful weekend, during which they paid a cool kind of courtesy to each other, Rachel could only feel relieved that he was going.

But he reached for her on Sunday night. And, in the middle of their desperate attempts to achieve some level of mutual satisfaction from their shared passion, he broke one of her strictest rules—he spoke to her. He asked her to forgive him. It made her cry out in pained protest at his spoiling what they were managing to share. Her wretchedness curbed his tongue, but when he came into her there was a new urgency about him that verged on the tormented, and afterwards she found herself desperately wanting to comfort him when he just turned and lay with his face pressed into the pillow, yet was unable to because it would feel so much that she was conceding something too important to him.

She only wished she knew what that important thing was! The trouble was, she was beginning to lose sight of what exactly was causing all the dissension between them.

Lydia, she reminded herself. Lydia.

Yet even that name was beginning to lose its ability to wound as deeply as it used to do.

Over the next few days she threw herself into a mad splurge of last-minute preparations for Christmas. She stubbornly ignored her continuing nervous stomach as she became engrossed in bedroom re-organisation until, by the evening Daniel was due home, she was beginning to feel so limp she wondered if giving in and taking to her bed might not be a bad idea.

They were all in the sitting-room, trying to erect the huge Christmas tree that had just been delivered, when the door opened and Daniel walked in. A rueful smile softened his harsh features as he took in the sight of all four of them struggling between the prickly branches of a disobliging tree.

'I see I'm still needed for a few small duties around here, then,' he mocked, bringing four heads whipping around in surprise.

The children deserted Rachel to fall on Daniel instead, and he, with a cry of mock terror, fell down on the carpet as two wiry bodies landed on top of him laughing and whooping, while the third member of their little trio had to crawl his way over to his father as fast as his hands and knees could take him.

Rachel watched, her hands pricked full of pine needles but unaware of the stings, smiling stupidly at the mini-war taking place on her sitting-room floor.

And it was there, on a sudden surge of the sweetest insight she had ever experienced, that she saw the blistering truth as to why her life was so worth keeping as it was.

Family. Family love. A simple yet complicated interconnecting weave of love, from one to the other to the other, that bound them all together so tightly that even when one link broke and tried to tear them all apart it couldn't. Because the others held on so fast.

Made it worthwhile to hold on fast.

And Daniel like this was the old Daniel. Not the one so rushed off his feet that he was too tired to take time out to wrestle on the floor with his children: to enjoy them—simply enjoy as they tickled him and made him shriek for mercy.

Michael sat on his middle, patting hard on the steel wall of a chest with both hands. 'I give in—I give in!' Daniel cried as Sammy straddled his shoulders to hold him down so that Kate could tickle him ruthlessly, the sly pair knowing Daniel couldn't do a thing to save himself while Michael sat squarely on his middle. 'Help me, Rachel!' he pleaded. 'I need help!'

She let go of the tree, watching it warily for a moment to be sure it wouldn't fall down on top of them all before she went to pluck up Michael, tucking him under her arm so that she could tease Kate with a bit of her own medicine, leaving Daniel free to deal with Sam. In one swift economical movement he was on his feet with his eldest son wrapped in a bear-hug of a grip while he rained noisy wet kisses all over his disgusted face.

'Yuk!' Sammy protested, wriggling like an eel and loving every minute of it. There were not many ways to give six-year-old boys the kisses and cuddles they needed but were not allowed to admit to. But Daniel was using the best way right now, by making a game of it. And by the time he set Sam down on the floor the little boy was flushed with happiness and pretending utter disgust. Then he was laughing shrilly as Daniel went after a squealing Kate. She was easy to catch; it was very hard to feign reluctance when all you really wanted to do was to be wrapped in those big strong arms and hugged and kissed.

Michael watched, his little face alive with the fun of it all. And Rachel hugged him to her, gaining comfort from his warm little body, when really what she wanted to do was beg for her turn as, once upon a time, she would have done—quite brazenly.

That Daniel was thinking along similar lines was clear when he set Kate down on her feet, then fixed his uncertain gaze on Rachel. Feeling suddenly shy and self-conscious, she handed him Michael, lowering her fine-veined lids over her eyes as he took the hint and rolled back down on to the floor to tease his younger son into infectious baby giggles.

The Christmas tree chose that moment to begin creaking warningly. Rachel reached it in time, but not before she became lost in pine branches. Another hand, longer and stronger than hers, appeared just above her own, Daniel's lightning-quick reactions allowing him to leap off the floor and snake out a hand to take the weight of the tree from her, easily pushing it upright again. Rachel then found herself being disentangled by firm but gentle hands.

'You've scratched your cheek,' Daniel observed huskily, and lowered his mouth to place his lips on the tiny mark by the corner of her mouth. His tongue flicked out to soothe the tender spot, and she quivered.

'Hello,' he murmured softly, grey eyes gently noting the blushing shyness in her expression.

'Hello,' she answered huskily, having difficulty meeting his gaze. Then his mouth was lowering again, demanding a slower, deeper, much more intimate kiss. He felt warm and vital, the hard-packed leanness of his muscled body so achingly familiar to her own. And she closed her eyes, giving herself up to the sheer uncomplicated beauty of the embrace.

The doorbell chimed, breaking them reluctantly apart as the twins shot off with a yelp to let Daniel's mother in, since she was expected at that moment.

'Y-Your mother is taking them to the Christingle service,' Rachel breathlessly explained.

'She is?' he answered absently, his eyes smoky as they roamed her blushing face. 'Good,' he murmured, and kissed her again, softly, tenderly, lingeringly, his warm mouth clinging to hers even when his mother walked into the room and halted abruptly when she realised what she was walking in on.

Rachel didn't even hear her. A love she had thought she had lost for good was welling up inside her, fanning a beautiful sensual warmth into every part of her tingling frame, and with a sigh that was like the soft whisper of a breeze against his mouth she slid her hands up his arms and curled her fingers into the silken darkness of his hair.

They were both out of breath when they eventually broke apart. Daniel turned to smile at his mother, but his vision was not quite focused, and Jenny Masterson's smile was unsteady as she gazed at them both with undiluted hope written in her anxious eyes.

It was only after Rachel had helped bundle the children into their warm anoraks, while Daniel secured the tree, that she remembered the reorganisation that had gone on upstairs while he had been away, and she bit down on her bottom lip, wondering how she was going to tell him and weakly putting the moment off until she had no choice.

They waved the children and his mother off together, Daniel's arm a possessive clamp around Rachel's waist as Jenny trotted off with Michael wrapped up warm in his push-chair and the twins skipping along beside her, chatting away nineteen to the dozen.

Daniel closed the door. The silence inside the house seemed strange after the noise of a minute ago.

'Come with me while I change?' he invited, tentatively offering her his hand.

She took it meekly, letting him pull her up the stairs behind him to their bedroom where Daniel gave a contented sigh and moved away from her to begin tugging at his tie.

Rachel watched him from the door, her hands twisting together in front of her. 'Er...' she began.

He didn't seem to hear, his steps taking him right into the bathroom. Then...

'What the——?' He was out of the door like a bullet, staring at her incredulously, thinking, she knew, all kinds of things which had to hurt.

'I had to put my parents somewhere!' she burst out defensively. 'This was the only practical solution!' She waved an agitated hand at their room, where the bathroom already stood shiny clean and empty of all their personal toiletries. She had emptied one of her wardrobes into Daniel's. It had been a tight fit, and she was ruefully aware that their clothes were going to need a good pressing before they would be fit to wear again. But...

'And where,' he gritted, 'are you and I sleeping?'

Her hand fluttered in the vague direction of the other bedrooms. 'It worked out quite well in the end,' she told him nervously. 'I had two new beds delivered, one in Sam's room and one in Kate's. Y-Your mother can sleep in Kate's room with her.' His mother always slept over on Christmas Eve—she liked to be there to watch the children open their presents on Christmas morning. 'I'll sleep in Michael's room and y-you can sleep in Sam's. It's only for two nights, Daniel!' she appealed for his understanding when he looked ready to explode. 'You know we daren't put the twins together or they'll never sleep! And as it is the children are quite excited about it. They——'

'Hell and damnation!' he exploded anyway. 'What is it with you, Rachel?' he bit out furiously. 'Why the hell should I give up my bed for your parents? Why can't they sleep in the other beds? Or have you done this just to get another dig at me? Because if you have, I'm warning you, I've damned well had enough of it!'

Rachel bristled at the injustice. 'Since when have my parents been any trouble to you?' she retaliated. 'You only have to put up with them once a year! Show them some consideration, for goodness' sake! They'll be driving down here tomorrow directly from closing the shop, and they won't stop until they arrive. They're big-framed, Daniel! And getting on in years. They won't feel comfortable sharing with the twins!'

'I can't believe you've actually done this!' he rasped, too angry to listen to a thing she was saying. 'I come home after one hell of a week in Huddersfield—Huddersfield, for God's sake!' he derided, as though it were the end of the earth. 'Looking forward to a peaceful Christmas in my own home—*my own* home!—and find I've been chucked out of my bedroom by a vindictive wife who can't find enough ways to... It wouldn't be so bad.' He changed tack on a blankly staring Rachel, running his angry fingers through his hair. 'It wouldn't be so bad if the damned house was big enough for me to get lost in if I felt like it. But because *you* refuse to move to something better, *I* have to lose *my* home comforts, *Me*!' he choked. 'A damned cash millionaire—living in a poky little cardboard box with three noisy little brats and a wife who...'

His mouth snapped shut, his angry gaze at last focusing on Rachel's blanched face, 'Damn,' he sighed. 'Damn, damn—damn.'

'W-Why don't you go to Lydia, then?' she suggested shakily, her throat swelling on the thickness of unshed tears. 'Perhaps sh-she'll give you a better time all round!'

Spinning, she ran out of the room before he could say another thing! He thought her vindictive! He thought their home a poky little box! And his children! Those dear, sweet babies who loved him so utterly—he called them brats!

She banged the children's supper dishes with gusto, soapsuds flying everywhere. She could have put them all in the dishwasher, but this felt better, giving her something to vent her anger on!

Two hands appeared on either side of her, effectively trapping her against the kitchen sink. And a warm mouth came down to nuzzle her nape. 'Sorry,' Daniel murmured. 'I didn't mean a single word of it.'

She sniffed, scrubbing at a plate that was in danger of losing its pretty flower pattern. 'Why did you say it, then?'

'Because,' he confessed, then didn't bother finishing, preferring to taste her throat instead.

'Because?' she prompted, hunching her shoulder in an effort to stop him.

'Because I was disappointed,' he rumbled. 'Because I've thought of nothing else but that damned bed all week—with you in it. Because I'd forgotten all about the problem with your parents and I felt guilty for letting it slip my mind. Because,' he sighed out heavily, 'I don't want to sleep in Sam's room. I want to sleep with you. I want to wake up on Christmas morning with your face next to me on the pillow. Because—oh, there are a hundred damned becauses. But they all add up to one thing in the end. I blew my top because you were taking away from me the only place where I feel close to you any more. I need that bed, Rachel. I need it.'

On a sudden sob, she dropped the plate she had been wielding back into the water and spun around to bury her face in his chest. 'Oh, Daniel,' she whispered, 'I'm so *miserable*!'

'I know,' he sighed, holding her close, letting the tears flow, stroking her back, his dark head coming to rest comfortingly on the top of her own. And once again his big frame became her rock, the place to run for the comfort she had always found given so unstintingly.

Eventually she sniffed herself back to some kind of calm, and Daniel pushed up her chin so that he could inspect the damage. She let him, as mute and petulant as Kate.

'My mother will kill me if she sees you like this,' he grimaced. 'One look at you and she'll blame me without even a hearing!'

Rachel smiled despite herself. But Daniel was right. Jenny invariably came down on Rachel's side in a dispute, whether she was right or wrong.

'Forgive me?' he asked, gently pushing a wispy tendril of soft blonde hair away from her damp cheek. 'Call a truce, Rachel,' he urged. 'Let's make this a good Christmas—hell,' he muttered, 'I'll even give up my damned bed if it makes you happy!'

'Who said it made me happy?' she objected, dipping her head so that she could rummage in his trouser pockets for his handkerchief, and having to suppress the urge to smile when her fingers brushed lightly down his groin so that he responded with a shuddering gasp.

'You provocative little witch!' he accused, knowing exactly why she had done it and ruefully amused by it. It revealed a glimpse of the old teasing Rachel—the one he'd thought lost to him forever. 'A truce, Rachel,' he pleaded huskily. 'Please.'

'You called the children brats!' she reminded him sternly.

'Did I say that?' He looked genuinely appalled.

'And more!' she complained.

'I wonder you didn't throw something at me,' he murmured contritely. 'Forgive me and call a truce?'

She pondered the suggestion, taking pleasure in the way his fingers were lightly caressing her face and throat. 'Are you really a cash millionaire?' she enquired curiously.

'Did I say that too?' His sleek brows arched. 'I must have been temporarily deranged.'

'Are you?' she insisted.

'If I say yes, will it gain me a bit of respect around here?' His smile was wry.

'It might do.'

'Then yes,' he nodded. 'You're looking at a cash millionaire—several times over, I might add, just to push up my rating, you understand.' It was said lightly, meant entirely as a tease, but it hurt something deep down inside her because she recognised that underlying the teasing was the real truth, that Daniel was indeed a very wealthy man and she hadn't even realised it. He was just Daniel to her. The man she had loved for what seemed all of her life.

'Truce?' he asked, lowering his mouth to nibble sensually at the corner of her mouth.

'Yes,' she mumbled, eyes closing in languid pleasure.

He lifted his head. 'Because of my millions?' he quizzed.

'Of course,' she smiled. 'Why else would I give in to you?'

He laughed, his manner at ease because, if he knew anything about Rachel, then he knew she was not mercenary. He dropped a kiss on the top of her head, then turned them both towards the kitchen door. 'Then come and talk to me while I change,' he invited, and led them both back up the stairs.

The bedroom was lit by its usual warm peachy glow. Daniel sent the bed a wistful glance as they passed by it.

'We can keep to our usual beds for tonight, of course,' Rachel remarked casually, and received a stinging slap to her behind for her tease, and they entered the bathroom laughing as light-heartedly as they used to do.

It was a nice Christmas, happy, relaxed, light-hearted— but soon over. And the time came for Rachel to decide if she was going to go back to Zac's class. Daniel made no comment, but his opinion was written all over his face whenever he caught her with her sketch-pad in her hands—which she in turn refused to comment on, simply because she wanted it to be her own decision with no manoeuvring from him.

So slowly, slowly, they slipped back to being guarded strangers in the same house. Rachel had to be aware that ninety nine per cent of the blame for this had to be because of their unsatisfactory achievements in bed. Daniel was a very sensual man, and her continued inability to give him all of herself challenged his virility. He hated the restrictions she placed on him: the darkness, the silence, the reluctance to go where their senses instinctively led them. And Rachel was afraid that if she didn't do something about it, then he might go in search of a fuller satisfaction elsewhere. Again.

Would that fear ever leave her now? she asked herself one morning, after a particularly disastrous loving the night before.

Daniel had been as wretched about his affair as she had been. But the knowledge that he could actually fall when the pressure became too great took away that necessary trust she needed to feel safe with him again.

Which left her with the most horrendous feelings of insecurity. An insecurity that played on her nerves to the extent that she was almost constantly plagued by an upset stomach that had never really improved in months.

The kind of months that started her thinking along lines that congealed the blood in her veins...

# CHAPTER TEN

Two o'clock Wednesday afternoon, and Daniel was gathering together the stack of papers he had been working on for his next meeting when the telephone on his desk began to ring.

'A lady on the line for you, Mr Masterson. She says she's Mrs Masterson?'

An icy shiver shot down his spine. Rachel never called him here. An accident? he wondered with alarm. One of the children? 'Put her through,' he commanded tautly.

By the time his secretary connected him, his mind had conjured up so many lurid things that could have happened to one of his offspring that he was momentarily confused when it wasn't Rachel's voice he heard speaking, quick with urgency, but someone else entirely.

He shook his head to clear it. 'Will you begin again, Mother?' he requested of that other Mrs Masterson. 'I'm afraid I didn't take a single word of that in.'

Within minutes he was in his car and heading at speed for home. His mother had the door open for him even as he climbed out of the car, and he strode quickly inside.

'She's in there,' Jenny told her son, her lined face crinkling with concern. 'She's so upset, Daniel,' she whispered tearfully.

His face clenched as he turned to open the door, to find Rachel huddled into the corner of the sofa. Her face was buried in a cushion, deep broken sobs racking her slender frame. He approached her carefully, his hands trembling a little as he shrugged out of his jacket and loosened his tie before attempting to touch her.

'Rachel?' he prompted huskily, squatting down in front of her and reaching out to clasp one heaving shoulder gently.

'Go a-way,' she sobbed into the cushion.

He frowned, puzzled and just a little frightened. He had never seen her like this before—so broken up that she couldn't even tell him what was wrong. And he remained where he was, gently rubbing her shoulder while he tried to think what could have caused her to break down like this? The name Zac Callum hit his mind, and his chest tightened on a hot band of anger. If that bastard had done this to her! If the swine had dared to hurt her when she was only just recovering from the hurt he himself had inflicted on her...

'Rachel...' He moved closer, running shaky fingers through her hair—and was shocked by the clammy heat emanating from her. How long had she been like this? he wondered. 'For goodness' sake,' he pleaded, 'talk to me! Tell me what's wrong!'

The tousled head shook. He swallowed tensely, not knowing what to do. Then, with a grim resolve, he got up to collect her firmly in his arms, then sat down with her cradled on his lap, cushion and all.

At least she didn't fight him, he noted, but just curled up against him with the cushion pressed against her face and kept on crying. He listened, his tongue cleaving to the roof of his mouth at the sheer bloody wretchedness of the sound.

'It's all y-your fault,' she sobbed out suddenly.

His fault. He sighed, casting his mind back over the past few days, trying to discover what he had done this time to cause so much distress. He'd thought he'd been particularly diplomatic over the last week or so. He hadn't said one word about her damned art class! He had not forced his body on to her more than he could possibly help. In fact, he'd stayed out of her way as much as he could ...

'Y-You were s-supposed to take c-care of it.' She damned him with that pathetically wretched voice which cut him to the quick.

He brushed his cheek over her hair. 'Take care of what?' he asked.

The sobs went deeper, threatening to choke her if she didn't calm down, and sighing, he took control of the situation, sitting her up and determinedly snatching the cushion away from her hot face. Her hands simply took its place.

'Calm down!' he commanded sternly, quietly appalled at the state she was in.

But, dutiful to that stern tone, Rachel tried to get hold of herself, dragging in some deep breaths that wavered heartrendingly. Daniel found his handkerchief, dragged down her hands, and gently wiped her tear-swollen face. She was so hot that he could actually feel the heat vibrating from her and, on another sigh, he stripped off the warm woollen jumper she was wearing, feeling her shiver as the cooler air hit her through her thin blouse.

'Now,' he said, 'let's hear what this is all about. You said it was something I've done, if I heard you correctly?'

She looked at him, her eyes swimming with hot watery tears. Her soft mouth wobbled, and Daniel almost smiled because she was staring at him through big wounded eyes much as his daughter would if she had not managed to get him to do what she wanted him to do. Only this wasn't Kate, he reminded himself grimly. This was Rachel. Rachel, who was no petulant child. She was brave and strong, despite that air of fragility she wore around her.

'Don't cry again,' he murmured roughly, when the tears began to run down her cheeks. 'Rachel, for goodness' sake—you have to tell me what's causing all this or how can I help?'

'You can't help! No one can help! I'm pregnant, Daniel! Pregnant!' she choked, then made a lurch for his throat where she began weeping all over again. She punched his chest with a clenched fist. 'It's all your fault! You said you would take care of it!'

He had been the one to 'take care of it' when she got pregnant with the twins! After that she had taken care of it—right up until she had developed a reaction to the Pill and had to stop taking it, so Daniel had taken charge again—and Michael came along!

'You're useless!' she spat at him, punching out at him again. 'You may be able to run a million damned companies!' she choked. 'But you're useless at everything else! I'm only twenty-five, for God's sake!' Her voice began to wobble again. 'At this r-rate you'll be nail-nailing down my coffin by the time I'm thirty!'

Now that deserved the smile it got from Daniel, but he pressed her face into his throat so that she wouldn't see it. 'Ssh,' he commanded. 'I'm still trying to take this in.'

But Rachel was angry now, and jerked into a sitting position on his lap to begin throwing at him all those self-pitying thoughts which had helped her to weep for such a long time. 'A proper little baby factory I've turned out to be!' she ground out scathingly. 'No wonder you keep me hidden away here under wraps, Daniel! Your big-time business colleagues would be shocked to discover what an efficient little production line you've set up in your own home! I bet——' she warmed to the idea '—if you put a team of your time and motions experts on me, they would have you up for contract abuse!'

'Shut up, Rachel!' This time he could not contain the need to laugh. 'I can't think while you're throwing all those crazy accusations at me!'

'Well, just think about this one!' she snapped, in a voice still thick with tears. 'I'm pregnant! And I don't want to be!'

Think on that as long as you want! she thought bitterly.

'How pregnant?' he asked after a long pause. He sounded tight-throated suddenly, as though the question had taken a lot of asking, and his face was suddenly white, that nerve in his clenched jaw jumping.

'Three months,' she told him, feeling a fool. Fancy not realising what was wrong with her—after all the practice she'd had, too!

'Three months,' he repeated, and the tension drained right out of him. 'Good God!' It hit him then, almost as hard as it had hit Rachel when the doctor had given her the news that morning. 'That means...'

'Yes.' She didn't need it spelled out for her; she could manage simple arithmetic. It must have happened the first time she had let him near her after she found out about Lydia, and everything went a little crazy.

'God.' He seemed stuck on blasphemies. 'I remember now, I never gave a thought to...'

Silence fell again, while they both pondered their own trains of thought. She still sat curled up against him, and Daniel was stroking absently at her hair. And suddenly it reminded her of another time when she'd sat with him like this, receiving those same soothing caresses while he came to terms with her news.

There had been no anger in him then. And there was none now.

'Well,' he said suddenly, 'that's it then.' He turned her face so that he could brush a kiss across her mouth. 'We'll *have* to buy a bigger house now. No bedrooms left in this one!'

With the twins—only they hadn't known then that she was having twins of course; that little shock had come much later, when she was more than five months pregnant—but with the twins, he had used a similar statement to announce his acceptance of his fate. 'We'll just have to get married,' he had said then. Same difference, Rachel thought with a mental shrug. Daniel had this capacity for accepting the inevitable.

She didn't go back to her art class. It was a decision reached entirely on her own. Drawing she had come to love again, but common sense told her that she would be doing herself no favours walking back into that class while Zac was still there. And although it was never mentioned by either of them, Daniel began taking her out on a Wednesday night—as if he wanted to compensate for what she had lost. But she did not stop drawing, and her sketch-pads could be found all over the house with their hurriedly drawn comical sketches scrawled in black on white paper.

They went house-hunting. And it took ages to find something which suited everyone. 'A case of too many cooks spoiling the broth!' she said drily to Daniel, after a weekend spent trailing around the local countryside viewing properties which did not suit one or the other's specific requirements.

'Why do you want something so big?' she complained once, when they'd arrived back home after viewing a huge mausoleum of a place that was just too grand for comfort. 'We may need something bigger, but not that big! It isn't as though we have to have all those extra rooms to entertain your business colleagues, is it?' He still kept a definite line between his home and his workplace and it still hurt her—hence the comment.

'We would have a damned hard job trying to entertain anyone here,' was his deriding reply. 'And I think, Rachel, that after all the hard work I've put in, making it possible for us to have virtually anything we want, you might allow me the pleasure of seeing something special for it!'

Then they found the ideal thing: an old manor-house built in warm red brick with long sash windows which let the natural light flood into the high-ceilinged rooms. It had its own acreage of land hemmed in by a six-foot-high brick wall lined with tall trees to keep the grounds very private. It suited Daniel's idea of prestige, and Rachel's idea of a home. The twins liked it because it had its own swimming-pool under glass at the rear, and stables. And, to clinch things, it had a small lodge-house by the electronically controlled gates which was ideal for Daniel's mother, who fell in love with the tiny cottage the moment she saw it.

It also had a ready-made live-in couple, who had been taking care of the house for over twenty years and were worried sick about what they were going to do once the manor-house was sold. Rachel's soft heart took them in and Daniel was happy to keep them because it meant fulfilling a couple more of his own requirements. They were getting a housekeeper to take some of the load off Rachel, and a gardener who was to double up as chauffeur and ferry the children to school and back every day instead of him and Rachel and the local taxi service doing it between them.

Rachel threw herself into the delights of completely redecorating and refurbishing their new home, and found to her surprise that she possessed quite a flair for it. She was carrying this new baby better than she had Michael, and, as winter fell away to spring, the new house began to take shape enough for them to consider moving in.

Daniel was up to his neck in yet another take-over—a small Manchester-based engineering company he had once worked for himself but which was now in deep financial difficulties—so he was spending more time up north than he was at home, while Rachel busied herself trying to complete the house-move before her pregnancy became too advanced for her to do it comfortably.

Lydia had faded into the background over the past months. She no longer haunted their lovemaking, though Rachel still needed the darkness to hide in if she was to respond to Daniel at all. But at least she seemed to be coming to terms with a betrayal that had almost wrecked their marriage.

Daniel's seven-year itch, she cynically referred to it in the privacy of her own mind. If the same thing did not occur for another seven years, then maybe she could cope with that. For she knew for certain that she could never leave him now. Her life was too much bound to him by their mutual love of their children and this latest addition soon to come. But love for herself? She dismissed that ideal as a dream which belonged to Rachel the romantic child and not this older, far more awakened· Rachel, who had learned to temper her emotions to suit their new relationship.

She was in their bedroom one afternoon when Daniel arrived home unexpectedly early from one of his quick trips to Manchester. He found her sitting on the floor surrounded by heaps of old clothes she was sorting out for jumble.

He looked tired out, and the way he glanced irritably at the mess told her that the never-ending sorting and packing was beginning to get him down. 'Why can't you employ someone to do all this for you?' he snapped out impatiently, shrugging out of his jacket and tie as he stepped carefully over the mess on his way to the bathroom.

'I'm not having strangers going through our personal belongings!' she protested. 'And how would they know what to throw out and what to keep?' she added sensibly. 'I have to do it myself!'

He didn't bother to reply, but the bathroom door shut with an expressive slam. A moment later and she was on her feet and rummaging for her sketch-pad. By the time Daniel returned to the bedroom, freshly showered and with just a towel slung around his hips, Rachel was sprawled across the bed with her pencil, busily drawing.

'What are you doing?' He came to lie beside her, receiving a scolding frown when he jolted her pencil.

'You cheeky witch!' he exclaimed when he saw what she'd drawn. Laughing, though, despite the fact that he could clearly recognise himself in the naked devil with horns and a forked tail taking a shower. But instead of water washing down over him, flames licked upwards while he stood there, wearing an expression of evil bliss. 'You cheeky witch,' he repeated ruefully—and filched the sketch-pad from her.

Rachel made a lurching dive to retrieve it, but he rolled on to his back, hooking his arm around her swollen waist to hold her still while he closed the pad, then began flicking slowly through the busy pages.

Rachel went very still, her heart thumping anxiously in her breast, watching his face intently as he studied each new sketch in turn. He wasn't laughing, but then he wasn't meant to. This was not one of Rachel's cartoon pads. And the only funny drawing in it was the one she had just done of him. No, this was her more serious work, until now kept right away from curious eyes.

The head and shoulders of Sam looked solemnly out on them from beneath faintly frowning brows, his hair ruthlessly flattened to his head as he insisted on its being. His chin was stubborn. He looked like Daniel—so much like Daniel that Rachel's heart contracted as she stared at him.

Kate looked pleased with herself, her golden hair a shimmering halo around her pretty face. She looked like the cat who had just stolen the cream—which she had, in a way, because that was how she had looked when she had just talked Daniel into letting her have a small pony when they moved into the new house. Kate had a mind of her own—stubborn, extrovert. She looked like Rachel, but she was not Rachel. She was too much her father's daughter for that.

Michael. There were more of him because he was the one Rachel spent more time with. There was one of him sleeping, with his padded bottom stuck up the air and poor old tattered teddy cushioned by his plump cheek. And one of him laughing, his small teeth standing out in his beaming round face. Then a serious one of him, face dark with concentration as he took that first wobbly step on his own.

'They're good,' Daniel said quietly.

Rachel took in a deep breath, her heart thudding now because she knew what was coming next. 'Thank you,' she said, and made a casual grab for the pad before he could turn to the next page. 'It gave me pleasure to do them.' She tugged, but Daniel was not letting go. Her nerve-ends began to tingle. He turned the next page— then went very still.

He had expected to see himself, she realised later. It seemed the logical conclusion to make when the pad was filled with drawings of the family. But it wasn't him.

It was her own face which gazed back at them. Rachel, with her hair a golden bob of fine-spun silk around a face that showed few lines of living. A young Rachel. A Rachel who had changed little over the years. Her mouth was small and soft, her nose delicately straight. But her eyes—those wide-spaced expressive eyes—looked out on them with a sadness in their gentle depths which tugged at the soul. To her it was like looking at a stranger. She had hated it when she'd finished it, could not see how accurately she had caught the sad, wistful creature everyone else saw when they looked at her these days.

And she had shown her distaste of the drawing by scoring a cross through it from corner to corner.

'Why did you do that?' Daniel asked sombrely, following one of the negative lines with a gentle finger which paused at the corner of her mouth.

Rachel sat up and away from him. 'She isn't me,' she said simply. 'I don't like her.'

He made no comment, but lay studying the drawing for a long time, while Rachel felt a touch of her old restlessness attack her and got up from the bed, pretending to return her attention to the mounds of clothes scattering their bedroom floor.

'None of me,' Daniel made wry note, when eventually he turned to the next page only to find the devil leering back at him.

Rachel's smile was forced. 'How can you say that,' she mocked, 'when that is exactly how I see you?'

She couldn't explain why she had never attempted drawing him. She understood why herself, but those reasons did not translate into words very well. Daniel was different. He was one of the family—yet not. The other faces in the book belonged—they were a part of her. Daniel used to be—the most important part of her— but he wasn't any longer. He had drifted away, become a blurred image in that place inside her where those drawings came from.

He didn't love her as the others did.

Daniel was the broken link.

She reached out to take back the pad, and he let her this time, watching her silently as she took it to store it away, in the bottom of her wardrobe, then closed the door on it before turning back to face him.

He was still lying on the bed, with only the towel covering the leashed power in his thighs.

'Where's Michael?' he asked softly.

Her insides curled. 'With your mother for the day.'

Their eyes held, and time stood breathlessly still in the quietness of the bedroom. He was asking something of her, his lazy eyes showing her the need beginning to burn inside him. She stood a mere arm's length away from him, nervous, unsure, blushing slightly, feeling the trailing beginnings of desire seep warmly into her blood, responding to the lean, muscular length of him stretched out on the bed.

Her gaze flicked down to the whorls of dark curling hair covering his wide chest, following restlessly the way they tapered like an arrow across the flat tautness of his stomach and disappeared beneath the covering towel. Daniel was tall, lean and essentially male, his legs two powerful limbs with long muscular thighs, and calves sprinkled liberally with crisp dark hair which she could actually feel rasp sensually against her own softer more delicate skin, even though she stood a good two feet away from him.

The sun was shining weakly through the window, and she realised with a small jolt that this was the first time in months that she'd openly gazed on his body like this. Her need for darkness had denied her this pleasure. Denied her the pleasure, too, of seeing the desire burn in his eyes.

His hand reached out, inviting her without words to come to him, and silently she placed her hand in his, drawn by a force too great to fight. His fingers closed around hers, being very careful not to break the hypnotising contact with her eyes as he slowly sat up and parted his thighs so that he could draw her between them. She was wearing very little, just a loose woollen dress and a pair of briefs. Daniel slid his hands around her thickened waist, then stroked them down her hips and thighs until he made contact with the hem of her dress.

She stopped breathing on an inward gasp. His caressing hands paused, his eyes dark and watchful, waiting to find out what that gasp meant. Then she was letting the air out of her lungs on a shaky sigh and her eyelids lowered, her soft lips parting as she bent to join her mouth with his.

He fell back and she went with him, her dress being stripped away from her body as they went. And, as quick as that, they were lost in each other, hungry, demanding, stroking and arousing in a sensual scramble of tangled limbs and intimate caresses and long, moist, drugging kisses.

She was ready for him—more than ready—as her senses began to draw together in that sweet, hot knot of need that made her pull him down on top of her, mouth urgent, hands clutching at the tautness of his hips in an effort to draw him deep inside her.

Then it happened. Loving him with every sense she had in her, Rachel allowed her eyes to open slowly, gaze into that stern, dark, beautiful face above her, see the sunlight play across his gleaming black hair, see the fierceness of his driving passion, his eyes glazed with the sheer intensity of it. Then the ghost of her hell came back to haunt her, and she snapped her eyes tight shut, whimpering in wretched frustration as her body began to tighten in rejection.

'No!' Daniel rasped, violence erupting inside him because he recognised what was happening to her. 'No, damn you, Rachel. No!'

She fought it, oh, she fought it with everything she could, her fingers clinging to him, her breathing fast and labouring with the struggle.

'Look at me!' he demanded raspingly, struggling to hold back from making that ultimate union. 'For pity's sake, open your eyes and look at me!'

Her lids lifted slowly, eyes taking their time to focus on his dark face locked with tension. His eyes were shot through with a hot haunted need she could not deny.

Daniel might not love her, but he desired her passionately—still, after almost eight years—still, when she was
swollen with his child—still, with, during and through
everything that had come between them over this last
six months. Daniel still desired her with a need that made
him tremble against her, and maybe that was enough . . .

'No!' he protested harshly as her lids began lowering
back over her eyes. 'No—you won't shut me out this
time, Rachel!'

His hands came up to take hold of her face, tightening
until her eyes flickered open in frowning confusion.

'You want me,' he stated fiercely. 'But you won't have
me unless you keep your eyes open and accept just who
it is you want! Me!' he stated harshly. 'Me, Rachel.
Faults and all. Me, the man I was before I let you down
so badly and the man I am right now!'

'And if I can't do that?' she whispered wretchedly.
'What if I can never accept what you did to us?'

'Then you'll never have me again,' he answered grimly.
'Because I know I can't keep on making love to a woman
who has to hide behind her closed eyes before she can
accept me inside her.'

He pushed himself away from her then, while Rachel
took in what he was actually saying. Daniel had just
issued her with an ultimatum, she realised as she watched
him stride back to the bathroom. He was telling her that
he had done paying for his crime. He was, in short, telling
her that she had to learn to trust him again or forget the
physical side of their marriage.

She couldn't believe it—found it incredible the expert
way he had just managed to turn the tables on her,
making her the one who had to make the concessions
from now on if there was to be a normal relationship
between them in the future!

Resentment simmered, boiled, then died when it came
to her that he could perhaps be right, and she did have

to accept him, faults and all, if their marriage was going to survive—which only threw her into further confusion about what she was going to do.

She was still floundering on the question a week later when something happened which tossed all her other troubles into oblivion by comparison.

The twins disappeared.

# CHAPTER ELEVEN

RACHEL blamed herself the moment she realised they had gone. It had been a week to top all weeks for tension in the home.

Daniel had gone into a cold withdrawal, making no effort to hide his anger with Rachel, so the whole household heaved a sigh of relief when he went off a couple of days later on a trip to Manchester.

But that wasn't all of it. It was the Easter break from school and the twins were at home all day. It didn't help Rachel's frayed nerves that they were excited about the coming move, that they seemed to be constantly under her feet, getting in the way so much that she caught herself snapping at them more often than was fair.

She was up to her neck in packing-cases when she heard the ring of the telephone and, on a muttered curse, she fought her way across the room on her way to answer it when it stopped.

That did her temper no good whatsoever, and her curses became richer as she fought her way back to where she had been working and got back to her packing again.

She was still grumbling to herself when Sammy and Kate sidled into the room. 'It was Daddy on the phone,' Sam informed her sullenly. He had not forgiven her yet for shouting at him for spilling orange juice all over the kitchen floor. He saw the scolding as an injustice because he had been getting the juice for Michael at the time, in his way saving Rachel the trouble, but Rachel had only seen the sticky orange mess she had to clean up and lost her temper.

'He said to tell you that he's on his way back from Manchester.' The small boy relayed the message with the same haughty coolness his father would have used in the same mood. 'And that he has to go into the office first so he will be late home tonight.'

Well, bully for him! she thought grumpily. Let him hide in his office while she did all the hard graft! Playing the martyr, Rachel? She heard the acid echo of Daniel's voice sound so clearly in her head that she actually jumped and glanced round, half expecting to find him standing right behind her. He was not, of course, but the taunt went reluctantly home.

'I asked him to come home and play with us instead,' put in a sulky Kate.

'And he, I suppose, put the phone down quick—in sheer fright!' She'd meant it as a sarcastic cut at Daniel, not at the twins, but they took it the wrong way, and Kate's face went red with anger.

'No, he didn't!' she cried. 'He said he wished he could play with us instead of doing stuffy work! And you're not a nice mummy!' she added heatedly.

Rachel caught a suspicion of tears in her daughter's eyes just before Kate disappeared, running back down the stairs with an equally disgruntled Sammy right behind her.

Sighing, she rested one weary hand on her swollen stomach and the other on her aching head, acknowledging that she'd probably deserved everything Kate had thrown at her, and fought her way back across the room to follow them down the stairs. The twins pointedly ignored her, pretending to be engrossed in the television.

She picked Michael up from the floor, where he had been playing quite happily with his bricks, glanced at the other two in the hope they would look at her so that she could say she was sorry, when they didn't felt irritation swell within her yet again, and flounced out of the room with her youngest, leaving them to watch their TV programme in peace.

An hour later and she was going demented. She had looked everywhere she could think of. But the twins seemed to have disappeared off the face of the earth! She had driven over to the park, hoping to find them playing on the swings. To Daniel's mother's house—knowing that Jenny was out for the whole day visiting friends, and equally sure that the twins did not know that and could well have walked around to her house in search of some sympathy and comfort. She had checked and double-checked the house, the garden and even rung the new house in the vague hope that they had somehow found their way there. But they hadn't, and she was just reaching the stage when she knew she was going to have to call in the police when the telephone began to ring.

She snatched it up, white with strain and trembling so badly that she could barely hold the receiver to her ear.

'Mrs Masterson?' an uncertain voice enquired.

'Yes,' she whispered through chattering teeth.

'Mrs Masterson, this is your husband's secretary...'

Her heart leaped to her throat. 'I-Is Daniel there?' she asked.

'No, he hasn't arrived yet,' the voice said. 'But your children have turned up here just now asking for him and I——'

'They're there?' Rachel cut in shrilly.

'Yes,' the voice assured gently, hearing her distress. 'Yes, they're here.'

'Oh, God.' An ice-cold fist went up to her mouth, stopping the well of tears. 'Are they all right?'

'Yes,' she was assured once again. 'They're fine—really.'

Rachel dropped down on the bottom stair as relief—blessed, blessed relief—took the strength right out of her. Then she was almost instantly up on her feet again.

'W-Will you hang on to them for me, please?' she whispered. 'I'm on my way. I'm—on my way...'

She dropped the phone, gave an odd, choked little laugh, then a single wretched sob, and then was rushing to go and get Michael.

Rachel arrived at Masterson Holdings just as the lunch-break was coming to an end, and the ultra-modern reception area was teeming with people on their way back to their respective offices.

Her cheeks flushed with rushing, eyes slightly dazed by shock, and still dressed in the same white stretchy leggings and one of Daniel's old pale blue work-shirts that she had been wearing all day, she came to a halt just inside the plate-glass entrance and stared bewilderedly around her while Michael did the same from his comfortable position on her rounded hip.

The children were nowhere to be seen. Her heart gave a sickening lurch and she started forwards, making for the reception desk she could see across the spacious foyer, where a pretty young girl sat flirting with a young man who was half sitting on the corner of her desk.

'Excuse me,' she interrupted a little breathlessly. 'I'm Rachel Masterson. My children. They——'

'Mrs Masterson!' The young girl came to her feet, her brown eyes widening as they took in every detail of Rachel as if she couldn't quite believe what she was seeing. Rachel didn't blame her—she knew she must look a sight—but neither did she care. She just wanted to see Sam and Kate—needed to see them.

'My children,' she repeated as the young man shot off the desk and almost to attention. 'Where are they?' she demanded, unaware that the receptionist's voice had carried right across the foyer and now everyone in it was staring curiously at her.

'Oh, Mr Masterson arrived not ten minutes ago,' the young girl informed her. 'He has them in his office and said for you to——'

'I'll take you up to him if you like,' the young man offered.

Rachel turned a distracted expression on him and nodded in agreement. 'Thank you,' she whispered, and followed him over to the bank of lifts, too distraught to notice the sea of curious faces turned her way.

The lift took them upwards, and ejected them on to a thick grey carpet that muffled their steps as they walked towards a pair of matt grey-painted doors. Rachel followed her guide more slowly, feeling odd inside, trembly and weak-limbed. The young man knocked, waited a moment, then opened the doors before standing back so Rachel could go by him.

She paused on the threshold, glanced warily at Daniel who was leaning against a large grey grained desk, his arms folded across his chest, flicked her gaze to the two woebegone figures who were sitting very close together on a long leather settee, felt the tears flood into her eyes, put Michael to the floor, choked out thickly, 'Oh, Sammy—Kate!' then fainted clean away.

She came round to find herself lying on the settee with something cool and damp across her forehead—and four faces with varying similarities about them watching her anxiously. She smiled weakly, and received four varying but similar smiles by return.

Daniel was squatting down beside her with Michael balanced on his lap and one of his hands warmly clasping one of hers. Sammy and Kate flanked him, leaning sombrely against a broad shoulder each. They all looked rather sweet like that, and she wished she had some paper and a pencil close by so that she could catch the scene forever.

'How do you feel?' Daniel asked in a gritty voice.

'Woozy,' she smiled ruefully, then turned her attention to the two runaways. 'I'm sorry,' she whispered painfully, and received two sobbing bundles into her arms.

They sobbed out their regrets, their apologies, their love, and their fear when they saw her faint. Then they were snuffling out the excitement of their adventure: ringing for a taxi, pooling their saved pocket money, arriving here to find Daddy not here and putting everyone into a panic.

'And frightening your mother half out of her wits,' Daniel silenced them dampeningly.

He looked hard at Kate, who lowered her head in mute contrition. 'It was all very neatly worked out.' Daniel took up the story. 'They rang the taxi firm you use to ferry them to school when I'm away,' he explained. 'Said you were sick in bed and wanted them bringing to me. They even produced one of my business cards with this address on to make it all look official.' He glared at Kate. 'All very slick,' he clipped. 'Very believable.'

'Oh, Kate,' Rachel said gravely, remembering how important Kate had felt when Rachel gave her the task of ringing the taxi firm to order a car to take the twins to school on those mornings Daniel wasn't around to take them.

But to abuse that bit of responsibility in such a way...!

The poor child's head sank lower.

'I thought of using Daddy's business card,' Sammy put in, gallantly prepared to share the blame.

But they all knew it was the more precocious Kate who would have thought up the whole thing. 'I'm sorry,' the little girl whispered, and Rachel saw with an ache her small hand lift to wipe the tears from her lowered cheeks.

The tension was rife, the fact that Kate wasn't going to her Daddy for a comforting hug telling Rachel that there had been some tough reprimands before she'd arrived.

Her gaze drifted to Daniel. He looked drawn and pale, his mouth a grim tight line that warned of a simmering anger. He held Michael against him, big hands spanning the little body as though he needed to feel the living comfort of this youngest child of theirs because he was too angry to give in to what was really troubling him— the need to hold the twins close too.

He caught her looking at him, and grimaced. 'My secretary is preparing some coffee,' he said. 'As soon as it comes I'll have her take the children down to the cafeteria for some lunch. Then we talk.'

That sounded ominous. Rachel dropped her gaze and eased herself into a sitting position, just as a young woman with a pleasant face walked in with a loaded tray.

Still holding Michael, Daniel got up and walked over to her as she placed the tray on his desk. He spoke quietly for a moment, then called the twins over. They snapped into action with an obedience that confirmed Rachel's suspicions that Daniel had issued a severe scold to both of them.

A moment later Michael was going trustingly into the other woman's arms, and she took the children out while Daniel turned his attention to the coffee.

He didn't speak, not until he had offered her the strong drink and sat himself down beside her to watch her drink the whole cupful.

'Right. What happened?' he said quietly then.

She shrugged guiltily. 'I've been impatient with them,' she admitted. 'Today perhaps more than usual. They were feeling neglected, I think—pushed away. So they went in search of comfort elsewhere.' She put down her cup when the tears threatened to come again. 'I thought they'd gone to your mother's . . . I searched everywhere for them . . . B-But it never entered my h-head that they m-might try to come h-here!'

'It's OK.' He covered her twisting hands. 'Don't upset yourself any more. They're fine. You've seen that they're fine.'

She nodded, fighting to get hold of herself.

'I'm sorry,' she whispered after a while.

'What for?' His head shot round to stare at her.

'For being a poor mother to your children,' she said. 'For intruding,' she added, 'here.'

'Sometimes, Rachel,' Daniel sighed impatiently, 'I wonder what actually goes on in that head of yours!'

'Did you smack them?'

He frowned at the abrupt change of subject. Then, 'No, I managed to control that particular urge,' he said drily. 'But that didn't stop my tongue! What they did was stupid, dangerous and downright wilful!' Angrily he shook his dark head. 'Sammy took his medicine on the chin, but Kate was appalled.' He grimaced. 'I don't think I've ever shouted at her like that before.'

'She'll forgive you,' Rachel assured him. Kate adored her darling daddy.

'Not if she's like her mother she won't,' he grunted, and Rachel lowered her eyes.

'It—it isn't a case of forgiveness,' she murmured. 'It's trying to forget it I find I can't do. You shattered my whole world, Daniel!'

'I know.' Grimly he looked down at their clasped hands. 'Shattered my own at the same time, if you must know. Not that that means anything.' He shrugged. 'I deserved it. You didn't.'

'Then why did you do it?' she asked in wretched bewilderment.

Daniel sighed, the sound seeming to come from deep inside his rigid chest, and he let go of her hand so that he could rake his fingers through his hair.

'Because she was there,' he answered brutally, and winced at Rachel's dismayed gasp.

'Y-You must have hurt her very badly.'

'Did I?' His mouth twisted cynically. 'She isn't of your ilk, Rachel. Women like Lydia have thicker skins. They don't hurt that easily.'

'And that makes it all right, does it?'

'No.' Hunching forward, he rested his elbows on his spread knees and stared grimly at the carpet. 'But I can't feel guilt for her hurt feelings when she gave no thought to mine.'

Rachel frowned at that, not understanding what he was getting at.

Daniel saw the frown and sighed again. 'If I try to explain it all to you, Rachel,' he offered, 'will you listen?'

Would she? Did she want to know? Could she take the full sordid truth of it? Her eyes drifted away from him, pained and bleak, soft mouth quivering with a vulnerable uncertainty.

His hand came out to cover hers, warm and strengthening. 'Please,' he asked again. 'You were and still are the only woman I have ever loved, Rachel. If you can't let yourself hear anything else, then, please—hear that, because it's the truth.'

'Then why Lydia?' she flashed, spinning her head back to lash him with her eyes.

His mouth straightened, the attractive curve of his lips becoming lost in the grim tight line. He took his hand away, letting it drop loosely between his spread knees. 'Because,' he said, 'for a short while last year, I lost control—not just with what was happening to you and me,' he enlarged, 'but here too.' His grey eyes skimmed the length of his plush office. 'Lydia was a safety-valve.

Pure and simple, very basic.' He fixed her with a grim look. 'I was under terrible pressure, and I used her, quite frankly, to relieve some of it.'

Was that supposed to reassure her? Rachel stared at him, the rumblings of anger beginning to bubble up inside her. 'So now I'm supposed to forgive—forget,' she said. 'And sit back and wait for the next time you're under pressure like that and feel the need to *relieve* it with some other accommodating fool who happens to be available?'

'No.' Unlike her, Daniel did not harden his tone. 'Because it won't happen again.'

The sceptical look she sent him was her opinion of that.

'It won't happen again,' he repeated patiently, 'because it didn't work the first time.' He studied her hurt and angry face to see if she understood what he was getting at, then allowed himself a small wry smile when he realised she certainly did not. 'You and your undying innocence,' he murmured drily.

'I stopped being an innocent, Daniel,' she derided, 'at the age of seventeen, when you took innocence from me!'

'You gave it, Rachel,' he corrected. 'You gave it freely.'

She flushed—couldn't help it because he was so damned right! And she hadn't just given, she'd virtually thrown herself at him.

'And, believe it or not,' he went on, 'I took when I'd had no intention of taking. No——' he reached out to grip her hands again '—don't take that the way I made it sound,' he begged. 'I wanted you, Rachel. My God,' he sighed, 'I *always* want you! But you were seventeen years old, for God's sake! And I was a reasonably experienced man of twenty-four! I knew that, in all decency, I should turn and walk away from you before things became too serious! But I couldn't,' he admitted.

'So I was determined to keep the relationship light—but I couldn't even manage that.' His jaw clenched momentarily. 'In the end, I found myself so obsessed by you that my work began to suffer. And yours did too,' he reminded her. 'You were heading for straight As in your exams before I came along. But instead of submerging yourself in study, as you should have been doing, you were out with me. And your parents began to get at me...'

Her eyes widened in surprise at that piece of news. She hadn't been aware that her parents had done anything but smile warily at him when Daniel used to collect her from home.

'They disapproved,' he continued. 'And rightly so. I was putting at risk all those years of schooling you'd already put in. And, because of you, I had put in abeyance all the big plans I had mapped out for my own career.'

'This?' she asked, meaning the office they were sitting in which made its own statement of his successful achievements.

He nodded. 'Or something like this.'

'So you fulfilled your dreams in the end, despite me,' she remarked a trifle bitterly.

'But at the expense of yours,' he added.

'Mine? How do you know what my dreams were if you never bothered to ask?' she queried.

'Art,' he stated. 'University first, then a career in art. Advertising, maybe, or design. It was all you thought about then.'

'Was it?' Her tone mocked his confidence. 'Which just goes to show how little you really know about me.'

His eyes flashed up to hers, dark and intense. 'Then what did you want?' he asked, and he swallowed tensely, as if he didn't really want to hear the answer.

Rachel derided him with a look. You, she wanted to say. All I ever wanted from life was you. 'Let's just say I probably got what I deserved,' she mocked instead, and knew the words hurt him.

'I was about to get out of your life eight years ago when you told me you were pregnant,' he went on grimly, and Rachel closed her eyes, accepting that it was his turn to hurt her. 'I'd spent that fortnight down here in London, if you remember,' he said. 'But what you didn't know was that I'd been attending a series of interviews for a job which would have taken me out of the country and as far away from you as I could get.'

She'd suspected it, Rachel thought wretchedly. Ever since Lydia had opened her eyes to what she and Daniel really were to each other, she had suspected her pregnancy had trapped him. Daniel had not wanted to marry her; he simply hadn't been given the choice.

'No——' again he grabbed her hands and squeezed them tightly '—you're mistaking my reasons. I didn't want to leave you!' he stated fiercely. 'But I was prepared to get out of your life for your sake! You were too young and had too much going for you for me to tie you down! The job offer was like a crossroads I had reached, and I accepted it because I believed it was the best thing to do for both of us! But it wasn't an easy decision and I was feeling bloody wretched by the time I got back from London with my cool goodbyes all rehearsed in my mind.'

He stopped, his eyes darkening on a remembered pain. 'Then there you were,' he murmured thickly, 'standing right in front of me, looking up at me with all that—all that...' He pushed a hand to his eyes, covering them for a moment with fingers which shook. 'And I stood there, dying inside because I was going to have to let it all go. The next thing I knew——' he swallowed '—we were making love when we should not have been, making things worse, because how the hell do you tell the woman you've just drowned yourself in that you're going to leave her?' he choked, too lost in his own pained memories to notice how still and pale Rachel had become. 'Then, while I was struggling to say the damned words, you laid your head on my knee and said calmly, "I'm pregnant, Daniel. What shall we do?"' He laughed softly, shaking his dark head. 'It was like being handed a reprieve with the hangman's noose already tied around my neck! I felt freed—alive—so alive that all I could do was sit there——' he spread his trembling hand out expressively '—and let the sheer bloody joy of it wash over me! I didn't have to let you go, because you needed me. You—needed—me!' he repeated hoarsely. 'I could dismiss your dreams of a career. I could dismiss your youth. And I could do what I'd really wanted to do and gather you in, keep you close so no one else would know what a wonderful, beautiful treasure I'd got!'

He sucked in a deep breath of air, then let it out again slowly. 'So, we got married,' he went on less emotionally. 'And came down here to live in that poky little flat in Camden Town. We had hardly any money, barely a possession we could call our own, but I don't think I've ever felt so happy in my entire life! Then the twins arrived, and I had a stroke of luck which gave me the chance to try something I'd always wanted to do. You know how I used to dabble in stocks and shares then?' She nodded. 'Well, after we married, I hung on to those I thought might bring in a good return one day, and one particular block did,' he said. 'It was my first real killing on the market, and I had a choice; buy you a nice little house with the money, or feed it straight back into the market. I fed it,' he confessed, as if it were a mortal sin.

Which perhaps it had been at the time, Rachel allowed, if only because he hadn't bothered to discuss what he wanted to do with her first. But then—she gave a mental shrug—perhaps Daniel would not be the man he was today if he had needed constantly to refer to others before he made a decision to take a risk.

'Then I spent the next few months feeling as guilty as hell when the flat became impossible to live in with two small babies and all the paraphernalia that comes with them. Then the stock began to pay big dividends, shifting up the market ladder at such a rate that I made my second killing in as many months! And after that——' he shrugged '—I never had to look back. We bought the house. I set up my own company, diversifying into helping out small ailing companies by gaining majority stock, then feeding more money into them to make them more efficient. And Masterson Holdings grew steadily, until it became what you see today. But not without its sacrifices,' he added grimly. 'The bigger the company got, the more time I had to spend working in it. And the sheer nature of my business meant I had to move in certain social circles if I was to keep an ear to what was going on in the business world. But the more I saw of that world, the more determined I became that none of its ugly taint was going to rub off on you! You were the rose-garden in the middle of the vile jungle I fought in,' he likened huskily. 'You were the only constant thing in my life. I would come home to you and see the sweet seventeen-year-old I first fell in love with, and I knew I would fight the very devil himself to keep you that way!'

He took another deep breath, his eyes hooded a little because he was revealing to her so much of the inner man he usually kept hidden away—the one she had been curious to know but had never looked closely enough to find for herself.

'I think someone up there must have known it,' he said ruefully then. 'Because the next thing I know you're pregnant with Michael, and not having an easy time of it. And one of my newest acquisitions becomes involved in a nasty little fraud scandal which takes months of legal battling to sort out. I'm away more than I'm at home where I should be, making things easier for you. You can be bloody stubborn sometimes, Rachel,' he inserted gruffly. 'We had more money than we could ever spend even if we tried, and you wouldn't let me hire anyone to help you.'

Her chin came up. 'If you can run this place singlehanded, Daniel, then surely I can take care of one small house and three even smaller children!'

He sighed, hearing the self-defence behind the attack. 'And we all have our limits of endurance,' he pointed out. 'You almost reached yours after Michael was born and he gave you hell for four months solid. And the twins developed a severe strain of measles.'

'And I found out about your affair with Lydia,' she added coolly.

But Daniel shook his head. 'No,' he said. 'That was the result of my reaching my limits of endurance, Rachel. I almost lost everything in the ugliest hostile take-over attempt I've ever heard of. Harveys—a bigger holding company than mine—decided it wanted me out of the running, and it went for me with every weapon it had. Including trying to slap a fraud charge on me.'

# CHAPTER TWELVE

'THE Harvey take-over?'

But she'd always assumed that it had been Daniel taking them over—not the other way round!

He nodded, unaware how new comprehension was holding her still with shock.

'It was bitter and it was bloody,' he said. 'And I had to take risks that made my mind boggle when I thought about them after it was all over. And where, at any other difficult period, I'd always had you to turn to for some blessed relief from it all, you were out of reach—tired and weak, and run off your feet trying to share yourself between two sick children and a very demanding baby and, selfish as I know it sounds,' he sighed out heavily, 'I resented the whole bloody lot of them! I needed you, Rachel! But you couldn't be reached! And—God forgive me—Lydia could.' He sucked in an anguished breath and let it out again. 'With Lydia's frankly brilliant help,' he conceded, 'I won the battle with Harveys. But for some reason that same God only knows, because I know I can't work it out, the relief of it sent me staggering over those limits of endurance I mentioned, and right into her arms.'

'How long?'

He glanced at her, his brows pulled into a puzzled frown. 'How long, what?'

'Did you have her as your mistress—how long?' she repeated rawly.

He shook his head, an odd expression twisting at the corners of his mouth. 'She never was,' he admitted. 'Not in the sense you're implying anyway. I have tried to tell you that once or twice,' he added wryly, 'but you refused so much as to listen, never mind believe, and—God knows,' he sighed, scraping his fingers through his dark hair, 'I didn't blame you. After all, I'd been unfaithful to you in every way but the ultimate act, indulging in my own light relief from all the pressures by taking Lydia out instead of coming home to you. Wining her, dining her...' His shoulders hunched as if the memory clenched at something vicious inside him.

'Mandy told me you were seen coming out of Lydia's flat,' Rachel put in huskily.

He nodded. 'After my battle with Harveys, I went a little crazy,' he confessed. She could see he didn't like admitting that; the self-contempt was etched into his rigid jaw. 'I just sat here and drank myself stupid until I wasn't fit to drive myself home. Lydia coaxed me into her car and drove me to her flat to sober up. Oh,' he added with a cynical twist to his mouth, 'don't get me wrong. She knew what she was doing and I knew what she was expecting of me when I let her take me there but——' he stopped to smile bleakly. 'In the end, I couldn't. She wasn't you and, drunk or not, the very thought of laying a hand on her made my skin crawl. She must have seen it,' he grimaced, 'because she just walked out of the room. I fell into a drunken stupor and awoke in a strange bed the next morning. Where she slept that night I have no idea, but she came back into the room just as I was struggling to pull myself together and trying to remember just what the hell I had done, already horrified and disgusted with my own behaviour even before she smiled and told me that I wasn't bad for a man with as much alcohol inside me as I'd had.'

He stopped to swallow and Rachel went pale, her heart dropping with a sickening thump to her stomach. 'She kept me wallowing in my own self-disgust for months before she told me the truth. It was her way of getting revenge on me, I think,' he said, 'because I took my business away from her and gave it to one of her partners. The night she spoke to you on the telephone was a vindictive attempt to hurt me through you. And the last straw as far as I was concerned. When I called her back I informed her that I was going to remove my business right out of her sphere. Now I'm talking real money here, Rachel,' he inserted grimly, 'a very lucrative account. And the fact that she had now managed to lose it completely was not going to sit well with her co-partners, which frightened her—so much so that she lost control of her tongue. The insults which flew between the two of us then were so vile they were unrepeatable, but one thing she did let slip, which went at least some way to making me feel better about myself—she told me I never touched her. Oh,' he added deridingly, 'not in those words exactly. She was out to slay and used the kind of insults gauged to cut a man's ego in half. But to me they were like music to my ears! I never touched her and, oddly, I knew suddenly that she was telling the truth at last. Knew because my own instincts had been telling me the self-same thing through all the weeks she kept me dangling on that tormenting string.

'And that——' he turned to look her directly in the eye for the first time '—is the full unvarnished truth of it—if you can bring yourself to believe it, of course, and I wouldn't blame you in the least if you couldn't.'

Rachel lowered her eyes, staring at her hands where they twisted tensely together on her lap. She wanted to believe him, needed to believe him, but . . .

'Money, power—you can keep them,' he ordained huskily. 'If I can have your forgiveness in return.'

'You already have that,' she told him irritably. But the doubts still clouded her eyes.

'Then what else do you want me to say?' he sighed in frustration. 'I cannot make your mind forget! Only you can do that.'

Impatiently she got up, angry suddenly that he was laying the problem their marriage had become on her. He had said a lot—revealed a lot—about himself, how he thought and felt. But none of it helped how she thought and felt; none of it revealed anything about the inner Rachel.

And maybe that was her problem, she conceded, feeling his eyes following her as she moved restlessly about the office. She, like Daniel, had always kept a part of herself hidden away. Dreams, he'd called them. But how was he supposed to know her dreams were fulfilled in him, in being his wife, the mother of his children, when she'd never actually said it?

Could she say it now? With all the hurt and misery she had carried around with her over the last months, could she afford to be as open and as honest with him as he had just been with her? To save what was left of their marriage, could she do it? Could—dared—she put her love on the line for him again?

Sighing into the heavy silence, she turned back to face him. Then she saw them, hanging in a neat row on the wall above Daniel's head. And her heart stopped beating.

Sam, Kate, Michael and herself. All professionally mounted and framed. Her very own sketches looking down at her from the wall of Daniel's office.

'I stole them,' he confessed, coming to his feet as she walked slowly towards them. 'I wanted them to look at whenever I needed—— Do you mind?' he asked anxiously.

Rachel was amazed she hadn't missed them! Then she remembered the turmoil still waiting for her at home and smiled to herself. She wouldn't miss a three-piece suite in that chaos! 'You've managed to get the cross removed,' she noted, staring at her own face and feeling oddly exposed by what it revealed. 'It isn't a good likeness of me.' She dismissed what her own eyes were telling her.

'It *is* you,' Daniel insisted. 'The real you. They all are to me,' he added, with a quiet pride which warmed her right through. 'Quite a family gallery, when you think about it.' He smiled wryly.

'Except you're not there.'

'No.' His smile died. 'Why is that, Rachel?' he enquired. 'Why was there no portrait of me in any of your books?'

He'd searched through them all? She hesitated over her reply, then told the truth. It was time for the truth, she accepted suddenly. The full truth. 'They all love me,' she explained, nodding towards the three faces of their children. 'I didn't think you did any more. I tried to draw you,' she added quickly, before he could say anything to that, 'but the features kept distorting so I gave up in the end...'

'Did Callum see these?'

'What?' The harshness of his tone threw her for a moment, and she had to think who Callum was. Then, 'Oh, no,' she replied. 'Nobody saw these other than you.'

'How serious did things get between you two?'

'It didn't get serious at all.' She shrugged Zac Callum off as though he were unimportant.

But Daniel wasn't ready to dismiss the other man. 'You kissed him!' he muttered. 'I saw you!'

'One hasty kiss in the front seat of a car?' she mocked his jealousy, then added softly, 'That's all it was—that's all!'

But he wasn't convinced. His fingers came to clench on her shoulders as he frowned darkly down on her. Rachel sighed, noting that he had managed to do it again and turn the tables on her so that she was having to defend herself against something that she had not even done! Then she smiled at the absolute ridiculousness of it all.

'You look like that devil again.' Her eyes twinkled at him. 'You know, the one who takes showers in vats of fire!'

'I'm going to kiss you,' he growled.

'What—here in your very office?' she mocked. 'Wrong setting, darling. I belong in your other world, remember?'

He kissed her, angrily and passionately. He kissed her until she swayed in his arms. He kissed her until her hands crept round his neck and hung on, fingers curling into the silken dark hair at his nape. He kissed her until her tongue linked sensually with his, and her breasts began to respond, and his own body pulsed urgently against the firm swelling wall of her stomach. He kissed her until she was breathless, gasping, eager, hungry and totally, utterly lost in him.

Then, 'I love you, Rachel,' he whispered urgently.

'I know.' Softly, she pressed her lips to his taut throat. 'I think I can let myself believe you again.'

He sighed then in gruff relief, and took her mouth again, kissing her long and slow and deeply.

One of his telephones took that moment to start ringing. Daniel turned to glare at it, then took hold of her hand and drew her with him over to his desk. 'Don't move,' he said as he let go of her so that he could reach out for the phone, then hitched one lean hip on the edge of the desk and barked out his name.

It was amazing how smoothly he switched from passionate lover to cool, collected businessman, she noted, hearing nothing of what he was saying as she curiously studied his face. He looked leaner somehow, more finely honed, as if his features had actually taken on a physical alteration to suit the man he was being now: sharp, shrewd, assertive. His eyes were cool—even though they never lost contact with her own. And his mouth was thinner, losing all that beautiful sensuality her kisses had given it.

She smiled ruefully, and he frowned an enquiry at her without faltering in the discussion he was having with his caller. And some little devil in her made her want to crack the tycoon armour, making her reach out to stroke a caressing hand along his thigh.

He almost choked on an inward gasp, his own hand coming to clamp fiercely on top of hers. The eyes flashed, the voice faltered, and Rachel laughed.

'I'll call you back,' he ground out, and slammed down the phone. 'That was an important client!' he accused, pulling her towards him. 'You did that on purpose!'

'I love you, Daniel,' she told him softly.

He went pale, swallowing. 'Say that again,' he ordered thickly.

Rachel reached up and pressed a kiss to his mouth. 'I love you,' she repeated, finding it easier now that she'd let herself say it.

Daniel inhaled deeply, his nostrils flaring as though he was savouring the very scent of the words. 'I've missed you telling me that,' he said as he exhaled again. 'I've missed having the light on your face when you say it.' He lifted a hand to her cheek, cupping it gently where the afternoon sunlight caressed her skin.

'I loved you when I was a child of seventeen,' she told him softly. 'And I've never actually stopped loving you since. It just got—bruised badly, that's all.'

'So you hid it all away and made our nights into torments of pure hell.' His chest lifted and fell on a heavy sigh. 'All those terrible silent lovings, Rachel. And the darkness.' He sighed at the pain of it all. 'Now there was a punishment. Those dark silent lovings.'

'Let's go home,' she murmured, wanting to hold him close, hold him against her, naked and gleaming in the light. 'Can you leave here just like that?' she then asked anxiously, remembering that all of this was, after all, his responsibility.

'I can do anything I like!' he claimed haughtily, straightening from the desk. 'I'm the boss. I own this lot!'

'Mmm,' she murmured. 'I'd forgotten that—cash millionaire, I think I recall you saying once.' Her blue eyes looked up at him speculatively. 'That means half your assets are mine if we get divorced. I wonder if it would be worth the——'

Taking her firmly by the shoulders he turned her towards the door. 'We're going home—to the new house, not the old one,' he said threateningly. 'Then we're going to dump the kids on our new housekeeper while we use one of the finished bedrooms so I can show you which *asset* of mine is more important to you!'

'Sounds interesting,' she mused.

'It will be more than interesting,' he promised threateningly.

'I am in a rather delicate condition, you know,' she reminded him.

'That never caused problems before.' He dismissed that argument. 'In fact,' he added silkily, 'I recall from past experience that you're rather more—sensitive at times like this.'

Just then the door to his office opened, and three children scrambled in, saving Rachel from having to refute that last provoking remark.

Daniel stooped to pick up Michael, who was falling asleep on his feet. The baby's head flopped on to his shoulder and Rachel smiled lovingly at them both.

They rode down in the lift and walked off towards the car park, Daniel carrying the sleeping baby, his free arm still resting possessively across Rachel's shoulders. Sam was a tornado fighter plane, bent on circling them all as they walked. Kate held tightly to her mother's hand. She had pulled Rachel's face down and kissed her a few moments ago, her blue eyes full of silent remorse. 'I'll never do it again, Mummy,' she promised solemnly. And Rachel knew she wouldn't. Kate had learned her lesson the hard way.

It was a sunny day, and half of Masterson Holdings seemingly happened to be gazing out of the office windows as their employer and his family made their way across the car park.

'I just can't believe it of him,' one man said. 'I knew he was married, but three—nearly four kids!'

'I've been working for him for years,' someone else put in. 'And I never knew he was married. He's always been such a ruthless swine, so sharp you could cut yourself on him. What the hell made a sweet creature like her marry a man like that?'

'He doesn't look so sharp and ruthless now,' the first remarked ruefully. 'In fact he looks kind of cute. Perhaps he's different at home.'

'Or maybe she's not so sweet and innocent as she looks,' the second leered. 'After all—four kids? That takes a lot of loving...'

'What about my car?' Rachel protested as Daniel herded them towards his.

'I'll get it delivered this afternoon.'

'Not while I have the keys right here, you won't,' she pointed out with perfect feminine calm.

Daniel muttered something beneath his breath, swapped the sleeping Michael for the car keys and commanded the twins to get in the back of the car. They scrambled in, he closed the door, then opened the front passenger door and carefully helped Rachel inside.

The faces pressed to the office windows watched him stalk back into the building only to reappear again a few minutes later with young Archer from Sales—the same young man who had escorted Rachel to Daniel's office earlier.

Daniel handed him the keys and pointed to the white Escort. The two men parted and Daniel climbed into the BMW. A moment later he was climbing out again and opening the rear door. The twins scrambled out. He came around to open the front passenger door and took the sleeping child from Rachel, then helped her climb out. Then they were all trooping across the car park towards the Escort, where words were exchanged with Archer, plus sets of keys, then the family were opening doors to the Escort and the reason for this swap became clear when the baby was strapped into a child safety seat. Archer was about to make for the BMW when he was stopped by Kate. She gazed pleadingly at her father, who glanced enquiringly at Archer, who shrugged and grinned and held out his hand. The daughter demanded her father's cheek for a thank you kiss, gave it, then was skipping off beside Archer and the rest were scrambling into the Escort.

'Good God,' someone gasped. 'They've got him wrapped around their little finger! I wonder what the formula for that is? It could be worth a fortune bottled!'

'Blue eyes, blonde hair and the most delicious body even while pregnant,' someone listed.

'I thought he had something going with Lydia Marsden not so long ago,' someone else murmured thoughtfully.

'Lydia Marsden!' the scathing cry went up.

'Sorry,' the other man shrugged. 'Stupid idea.'

'Nice kids,' someone said.

'Nice wife,' said another.

'Nice car,' laughed the next.

'Nice home?' The joke continued down the line.

'Nice business,' sighed someone wistfully.

'Nice dole queue if you don't get back to work!' shouted out a voice which drowned out all the rest.

'Remind me to have a safety seat fitted into my car, will you?' Daniel muttered as he climbed behind the wheel of the Escort and readjusted the seat to fit his longer frame.

'What—and ruin your macho ruthless tycoon image?' Rachel mocked.

'What macho ruthless tycoon image?' he derided. 'Did you bother to look up at the windows in my building?'

'No—why?' She turned to look now, though, saw the long row of curious faces and blushed hotly. 'Will they tease you about us?' she whispered anxiously.

'Not to my face, if they have a healthy sense of self-preservation,' he grunted, then sighed. 'Though God knows what they'll say behind my back.'

'Never mind.' Rachel put a comforting hand on his thigh. 'We all love you. Macho ruthless tycoon or not.'

'Keep your hand where it is,' he muttered tensely, 'and I'll be labelled a damned sex maniac!'

'What's a sex maniac?' a young voice enquired from the back.

Rachel choked back a giggle and snatched her hand away. Daniel looked heavenwards and sighed. 'When you're older, son,' he answered drily. 'I'll explain when you're older.'

'Will you explain it to me when I'm older too?' Rachel asked guilelessly.

His eyes flashed her a burning look. 'I'll do better than that. I'll show you just as soon as I can get you alone!' he promised.

'With the light on, so I can——'

'Don't, Rachel!' he groaned, closing his eyes on a spasm of pain. 'You don't know how much I want to do that.'

'Yes, I do,' she said, and her eyes told him why.

Daniel's darkened. 'Just hold that thought,' he commanded, and put the car into gear.

## UNLOCK THE DOOR TO GREAT ROMANCE
## AT BRIDE'S BAY RESORT

Join Harlequin's new across-the-lines series, set in an exclusive hotel on an island off the coast of South Carolina.

Seven of your favorite authors will bring you exciting stories about fascinating heroes and heroines discovering love at Bride's Bay Resort.

Look for these fabulous stories coming to a store near you beginning in January 1996.

**Harlequin American Romance #613 in January**
*Matchmaking Baby* by Cathy Gillen Thacker

**Harlequin Presents #1794 in February**
*Indiscretions* by Robyn Donald

**Harlequin Intrigue #362 in March**
*Love and Lies* by Dawn Stewardson

**Harlequin Romance #3404 in April**
*Make Believe Engagement* by Day Leclaire

**Harlequin Temptation #588 in May**
*Stranger in the Night* by Roseanne Williams

**Harlequin Superromance #695 in June**
*Married to a Stranger* by Connie Bennett

**Harlequin Historicals #324 in July**
*Dulcie's Gift* by Ruth Langan

Visit Bride's Bay Resort each month wherever Harlequin books are sold.

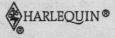

Where there's a will there's a way...
for four charismatic characters to find true love

## by Sandra Marton

When Charles Landon dies, he leaves behind a different
legacy for each of his children.

As Cade, Grant, Zach and Kyra react to the terms of
their father's will, each receives an unexpected yet
delightful bequest:

A very special love affair that will last a lifetime!

Watch for:

Cade's story: *An Indecent Proposal*—
Harlequin Presents #1808—April 1996

Grant's story: *Guardian Groom*—
Harlequin Presents #1813—May 1996

Zach's story: *Hollywood Wedding*—
Harlequin Presents #1819—June 1996

Kyra's story: *Spring Bride*—
Harlequin Presents #1825—July 1996

Harlequin Presents—you'll want to know what
happens next!

Available wherever Harlequin books are sold.

# HARLEQUIN  PRESENTS®

The latest in our tantalizing new selection of stories...

## *Wedlocked!*

### Bonded in matrimony, torn by desire...

#### Next month watch for:

***Ruthless Contract*** by Kathryn Ross
Harlequin Presents #1807

Locked in a loveless marriage. Abbie and Greg were
prepared to sacrifice their freedom to give Abbie's adorable
nieces a stable home...but were determined that their
emotions wouldn't be involved.

Then fate stepped in and played her final card, and
the ruthless contract between Abbie and Greg became a
*contract for passion.*

Available in April wherever Harlequin books are sold.

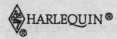